NEGATIVE RETURN

A DURGA SYSTEM NOVELLA

JESSIE KWAK

NEGATIVE RETURN

A DURGA SYSTEM NOVELLA

JESSIE KWAK

For Robert,

for always pushing me to write my best.
And for watching all those gangster movies with me.

1

BAD JAZZ

The lounge singer is in over his head.

He has a decent voice when he stays in the right register, Manu Juric thinks, but every song he's chosen tonight has been a challenge — a touch too high, the notes fraying around the edges. The Bronze Room is too cheap a bar to filter it through an autocorrect unit.

Manu'd chip in to buy them one, but he'll never get invited back after what he's about to do.

The singer's crooning in a mismatched suit, his hair and makeup done expertly but cuticles scuffed and shoddy, nails flaking underneath the cheap lacquer. Not just overreaching his vocal chords — he's overreaching his league.

Manu tipped him anyway, earlier this evening, his tagged one-mark token tumbled in with all the others in the jar.

Manu's drinking whiskey, the bar's cheapest over plenty of ice to water down the flavor of engine oil. He's sipping it slow, taking his time, and already he's starting to get looks from the bartender.

Nobody nurses shitty whiskey at the Bronze Room. The bartender is one poorly sung verse away from calling his boss and reporting his suspicions.

Manu knocks back the whiskey, tags the bottom of the glass, then raises a finger to the bartender. The bartender slides another whiskey across the bartop; Manu thanks him with a wink and a bit too lingering of a smile — it's not faked, there's plenty to admire, and the bartender's tight shirt doesn't require much of the imagination. Manu transfers him a generous tip from Sylla Mar's expense account.

The bartender just turns away with a polite service-industry smile and drops Manu's empty glass into the sanitizer without noticing the tag at the bottom. Let him come to the wrong conclusion about why Manu is camping at his seedy bar just outside the posh, touristy Tamarind District.

Manu can't even remember the last time he came to this part of Bulari. He thinks it was when he was still a kid, just dropped out of third levels to help his dad with the business, barhopping on cash stolen from his dad's till with some of his buddies from Carama Town, tallying up who could get the most colorful cussing-outs from tourist girls and toss-outs from bouncers. If he remembers right they got kicked out of six bars before the cops got called.

It was a good night.

Manu gives the Bronze Room another scan. This may have been one of those bars; he can't remember. The end of that night's a bit of a blur.

Manu taps a fingernail against the side of his glass, waiting. His nails are a poison acid green tonight, same as his hair. The color pops nicely against his black skin.

He goes over the dossier once more.

The mark tonight's on the meaner end of the Bulari thug spectrum; he's the type almost everybody'd like to see gone, though nobody but Manu's been stupid enough to try. Small crew of riffraff, each uglier and crueler than the next. Got himself a live-in lady, a clean-looking type who must have a pretty low opinion of herself to end up with scum — but she's hardly alone in this city. Manu'll be doing her a favor, killing Willem Jaantzen.

Manu's been gathering intel on his mark for two weeks, long enough that Sylla Mar's started dropping hints that maybe his heart's not really in it, that maybe Manu's all talk and no action.

Those are the exact words she used, too, last time her goons brought him in. Lounging on that black velvet like she styles herself a goddess, smoke from her laced cigarette spiraling through her neon purple and pink locks. Dry, over-painted lips and eyelids weighed down with pigment, Sylla looked a caricature of a vid crime lord, right down to the thick-jowled musclemen who flanked her divan.

Even now, Manu tries to imagine those men as his co-workers, Sylla as his boss. Tries to imagine himself taking orders spoken in that husky undertone, punctuated by the cartoonish cracking knuckles of her goons.

Wonders if he'll ever stop watching his back with them as his crew.

No. Joining Sylla's crew isn't ideal, but who ever said life was perfect? The city's getting tight, lately. Strangling out the independent operators, choking out the way Manu used to exist. Too many petty alliances between the bosses, too many turning snitch on the little guys to build up their credibility with the government. Sometimes a freelance hitman needs a friendly crew to weather out the storm of crackdowns and backstabbings.

And Sylla's crew will do.

Better than getting himself an indenture. Manu'd rather be free and hungry than owned by some corporation.

Provided he can handle this initiation she set out for him.

Killing Willem Jaantzen.

It's a terrible idea, and Manu's been thinking of walking away all week. He actually can't decide if Sylla's messing with him — maybe she's one of those women who hates saying no outright, and this is just a convenient way to get rid of him for good rather than taking him in. She sure didn't seem to think he could actually do it.

If he's honest with himself, he hasn't been thinking he can do it, either. He's taken out his fair share of lowlifes and dead-beat ex-boyfriends, but he's never had a mark this big.

You don't know if you don't try, though, right?

Because if he makes this hit, it doesn't even matter if he sticks with Sylla and her band of shifty thugs. Killing Jaantzen will get him a job wherever he wants.

Killing Jaantzen with style might even get him a job with Thala Coeur, Blackheart herself. Now there's a scary bitch — but she's got a crew that actually watches out for each other. Joining Blackheart's crew, now that's a proper life goal.

Manu doesn't need Sylla, but he does need this win.

The singer stops crooning to a smattering of applause that

seems more grateful than appreciative, and he disappears into the back with his tip jar. Manu notes that with a frown. It's not a big deal — Manu's tags have been thoroughly seeded. Just, Manu hopes the singer hasn't put all those tokens in his pocket. Nobody deserves that, even for botching show tunes this badly.

Manu takes another sip of shitty whiskey.

He's gonna have fun busting this place up.

Manu doesn't need to be watching the door to know when Willem Jaantzen walks in. The whole energy of the place shifts, gets thin and sharp as a razor. There's two Arquellian girls a few seats down the bar, laughing too loud to hide their nerves, racking up stories of slumming it in Bulari to tell their friends back on Indira. They notice the hush but don't mark its meaning; the one closest to Manu glances towards the door and raises a catty eyebrow before turning back in a cascade of black ringlets to whisper in her friend's ear.

Manu shifts like he's checking her out and sees Jaantzen walk past, all broad shoulders and barrel chest. He's dressed more stylishly than Manu's used to seeing, like a man taught young which social cues others respect and who's now able to afford it. He's got two silver earrings in his right ear, two silver rings on each hand — bright glimmers against his rich brown skin.

Jaantzen ensconces himself at an empty table, though he doesn't seem possessive about it, not like Manu expects from a man at the head of one of Bulari's most up-and-coming crime rings. It's not the best table in the house, but it's in the corner with a decent view of the door. And a proximity to the stage Manu's sure Jaantzen will regret when the singer comes back for his next set.

Jaantzen's not traveling with bodyguards, this deep in his own territory, but he does have companions. Manu recognizes them: a brother and sister pair a lot of Bulari's bosses work with, the Lordeurs. They're bankers, kind of. Laundering big takes and fencing stolen goods. Tossing money out and reeling it back in with fat fish like Jaantzen attached.

He hesitates now. You never know when you might need a loan — plus, the Lordeurs've got a lot more friends than a loner thug like Jaantzen. Manu wonders if he'll ever need their services, decides probably not. And anyway, the whole bar is tagged at this point. If he walks away now he's never getting another chance — and he's out a small fortune in hornet tags.

Manu ignores that nagging, rational voice telling him that the smart thing to do is to walk away.

The singer's gone back up onstage; Manu catches Jaantzen's frown of annoyance at the first warbled notes, catches the singer's furtive glances at Jaantzen's nearby table. The boss is in the house tonight, and this guy knows he's not getting invited back for another gig.

Manu pushes his glass back towards the bartender and waves off the raised eyebrow asking if he wants another drink. He slips his little transmitter underneath the bartop and clicks the sequence to arm it. Feels it pulse faintly under his fingertips to tell him it's good to go.

No safe return now. Not until he kills Jaantzen.

Manu pushes off to the bathroom, a touch of whiskey sway to his shoulders and a sloppy nod to one of the Arquellian girls. She gives him a dirty look.

He's counting, and as he draws level with Jaantzen's table — a fraction of a second after he hits twenty — the bar shatters. The front of the glasses case blows off its hinges in a rush of smoke and fire. The long mirror beside the bathroom hallway and the picture window beside the front door both shatter, cascading shards of glass hitting all the high notes over the sound of screaming. At the back of the stage, the singer's backpack explodes. That's where that tagged coin ended up; Manu lets the thought slide past.

His attention is entirely on Jaantzen.

The Lordeur siblings have ducked to take shelter below the table — the little blasts from the hornet tags sound like gunshots, and all around people are diving to the floor.

Willem Jaantzen is not diving to the floor.

He hasn't registered Manu as the enemy yet — Manu dropped like the others in the chaos. As Jaantzen turns away to scan his bar, weapon in hand, Manu takes his shot.

Jaantzen must have heard something, seen a flash. Anyway, he's fast for such a big man, and as Manu squeezes off a second shot, Jaantzen kicks the pistol out of his hand.

No worries, Manu's got a backup gun.

He draws it, springs back to his feet and away as Jaantzen charges him, feeling the situation slip. Had to be flashy to impress Sylla, he thinks. Had to be an idiot.

His third shot is an inch too low, hits square in Jaantzen's body armor rather than in the throat, and Jaantzen only grunts, catches him with an elbow to the sternum, a meaty

7

hand to the throat. Jaantzen lifts him off the ground by his collar, those dead shark's eyes searching his, and all he can think is that he's seen this scene in gangster vids, and it does not end well for the guy with his feet dangling over the glass-strewn bar floor.

Jaantzen lifts his chin to someone behind Manu, and a blast of pain hits him between the shoulder blades.

Game's over.

2

BOTCHING THE JOB

Manu is surprised to wake up.

That he's bound to a chair in an empty base-ment, single bulb sputtering overhead — that's not so much a surprise. Jaantzen hasn't killed him, so this is definitely the sort of place he'd find himself.

The floor around him is covered in tarps, a bad sign. But he's still dressed, and he's not gagged, so . . . Manu scents the possibility of negotiation in the air.

Footsteps behind him, two pairs. "I'll answer anything you want," he says, conversational. Let's start off on the right foot here. Let's be helpful.

"Giving up so easily?" He's been studying that voice for weeks: Willem Jaantzen.

Manu shrugs. "Nothing to give up," he said. "I ain't got nobody to protect."

"Working on your own, then," Jaantzen says.

"I don't like working with others," Manu says. "I end up pulling all the weight, but you still gotta split the profits with the team. Or one of the other guys pulls a gun." No point in mentioning Sylla Mar — she's not big news enough to get him out of this mess, even if he could live with himself for snitching. He may not give a shit about her, but he's got morals, dammit.

"You could pull the gun first." A footstep, crinkling in the tarps.

"Guess I never think of that."

"Shortsighted."

"Or longsighted," Manu says. "Could be I'm building up a rep as somebody folks want to have around. I hear I'm easy to work with." He wants Jaantzen to step out in front of him. Partly to look the man he couldn't take down in the eye, partly to read what chance he's got of getting out of this alive. "You got a gig?"

A long pause. "I'm sorry?"

"A gig. You need some work done?"

"You think I'm going to hire a man who just tried to kill me?"

"Papa always said I had too many big ideas for my own good," Manu says.

"I'd say your father was right," Jaantzen says, but there's a hint of amusement in his voice that Manu reads as a good sign. "What's your name?"

"Manu Juric."

"Manu. Juric." Jaantzen rolls the words around on his tongue like he's tasting them. "How much am I worth to you dead, Mr. Juric?"

"Five hundred thousand marks," Manu says. It's not what Sylla would've paid him — she's too stingy — but he's seen that number floating around the bounty boards. It's a mouth-watering amount, but it hadn't been enough to get Manu to jump into this mess earlier.

Should've kept that cautious mindset, it seems.

Jaantzen whistles low. "A tempting sum. I can see why you let it make you careless."

Manu bridles at that, but bites his tongue. You don't get very far mouthing off to the bad guy when you're chained to a chair in his murder dungeon. Manu may have been dumb to try for this bounty, but he's not an idiot. Not normally.

"Five hundred thousand marks has a nice ring to it," he says.

The tarps rustle again; a footstep to the right. Jaantzen appears in Manu's peripheral vision.

"Tell me about yourself, Mr. Juric. I don't believe I've heard your name around."

Manu licks his lips. "I'm a bounty hunter. Freelance hitman. You got a job needs done?"

"Depends. Do you normally botch your hits so badly?"

"Touché, man."

"How's your résumé, Mr. Juric? Anyone I've heard of?"

Manu's thinking hard about the string of lowlife scum he's taken out over the years, but he's coming up blank in regards to notoriety. "The list is long, but it's not very distinguished," he finally says.

Jaantzen just tilts his head; the light from the sputtering bulb glints off his silver earrings. "How long can the list even be? You're what, eighteen?"

"C'mon, man. Twenty-four. But I seen your rap sheet from when you were eighteen, so I'd guess you know what even a teenager can accomplish with the right attitude."

Jaantzen's eyebrow arches. Manu tries to act like he didn't mean it as a challenge, like he's just making conversation in a charming murder dungeon. His shoulders are starting to ache, a low scream he's doing his best to ignore. The way Jaantzen's watching him, Manu can't tell if he made a serious tactical error there.

Finally Jaantzen looks past him, nods sharp to whoever's waiting over Manu's left shoulder. Manu tenses, but no blow comes.

"You're a middling hitman, Mr. Juric," Jaantzen says, but it's not an insult — Jaantzen's musing something over. "But you do create an impressive distraction. And I can be more valuable to you alive."

"You'll pay me half a million marks? For what?"

"Let's not start with the sum. After all, I still need to pay for repairs on my bar." There's a speculative chill in Jaantzen's eyes. "Let's start with me not killing you."

"Pretty valuable, that." Whoever's waiting over Manu's left shoulder takes a long, deep breath through his nostrils; Manu can't shake the feeling that the man's scenting his fear. Manu tries harder to force his heart rate back down. "My life's a good start."

Jaantzen tilts his head, watching. He's lit from behind, only the stern curve of his cheek, the regal angle of his nose lit by glancing light. "Excellent."

A footstep to Manu's left; the second man finally comes out from behind him. Manu's been picturing a clone of

Jaantzen, but while the man's just as huge, he's uglier and fair-skinned, his mane of black hair glossed back into a ponytail. Manu fights the urge to laugh inappropriately, but this hunk of muscle is just the spitting image of the disposable, bad-tempered goons Jaantzen's known to run with.

"Meet Kai," Jaantzen says. "He's running the team."

Kai cracks his knuckles like he read it in the Ultimate Manual of Intimidation Tactics. Dammit, Manu hates working in teams. But beggars can't be choosers — not the way the game's being played these days, and not when a goon with fists the size of your head is looking for an excuse to use them.

"Nice to meet you, Kai," Manu says.

"That's the spirit, Mr. Juric. Now. Are we doing business?"

Manu nods, wrists burning. "You got it, boss."

"Good," says Jaantzen. "Kai?"

And he turns and walks out of the room, nonchalant. Manu takes a deep breath. He supposes he deserves this.

The big man steps forward with a smart punch to the ribcage, another to the gut, Manu doubles in the chair, retching. A fist to the jaw snaps his head back, and for a dizzying moment he's about to black out. A thick hand grabs him by the back of the neck, shakes him roughly out of the fog. "You listen to me," the man says. His voice is close in Manu's ear, his breath is a patina of mint over halitosis.

"Listening." Manu's aware that the word comes out as an embarrassingly frantic gasp.

"You answer to me, you got that?"

Manu nods. He thinks this has been abundantly clear

from the beginning. The theatrics weren't necessary, but he understands the intimidation game.

Or, he thinks he understands the game.

A knife flashes into Kai's fist, and for a moment Manu thinks he's dead. That all this talk of jobs and money has been a weird sort of foreplay to the main event. What else could he expect? He's heard the rumors about Jaantzen. The man attracts only the sickest lowlifes too unbalanced to find a home in any other crew.

Kai tilts his head, raises the knife. "When you look in the mirror, what do you see?" The knife presses the length of Manu's cheek, a thin, biting line.

Manu's stomach clenches in fear. He can't answer.

"What do you see?" A touch harder on the blade. Manu's thinking about nothing but his left eye, that gleam of metal bisecting his vision. His left eyelid is squeezed shut tight like that scrap of flesh would do anything to protect the eye beneath.

"Just a kid from Carama Town," Manu says carefully, trying not to move.

"Not anymore." The knife slips — just a hair's breadth — and Manu feels something warm and wet trickle down his jaw. "You look in the mirror now, you see somebody belongs to me," Kai says. "You got a question about this gig, you talk to me. You get an order from Jaantzen, you check with me first. I find out you didn't, I kill everyone you have ever cared about. We clear?"

Manu nods, as carefully as he can.

"We clear?"

"We clear."

Another flash of the knife, and the ropes around Manu's arms fall free. He resists the urge to touch his stinging cheek — it doesn't feel deep, though he can feel the trickle of blood slowly dampening his collar.

"Good," says Kai. "Now let's go meet the rest of the crew."

3

MOTLEY

Manu's new friends are waiting for him inside a cavernous warehouse. Kai blacked out the spinner's windows on the way here, but they're somewhere near the docking yards, Manu thinks. He can feel the building shudder as one of the larger cargo haulers takes off rumbling into orbit. It's midday — Manu wonders just how long he was out — but he can't see a thing out the warehouse windows. They're all too high and smoky, light filtering thin and miserly through them.

The warehouse is set up like an ops center: screens and desks, cots lined up like they expect everyone to settle in for a few days. Manu can feel his neck cricking already as he frowns at the narrow beds.

"Make yourself at home," Kai tells him.

"Where's my gear?"

Kai just walks away from him, and Manu doesn't press it.

Kai's twice again Manu's weight, and he didn't get that way by sitting around eating fritters. Jaantzen hasn't followed them up the stairs, and Manu isn't sure whether he feels more comfortable with Kai alone or with the mob boss around.

Neither, he decides. Definitely neither.

Fortunately, now he's got more options when it comes to dance partners.

There are four others in the huge space. A hook-nosed man is squinting at his comm like he's working, but the jerk of his shoulders and faint grin on his bruiser's mouth betray his game. When the man sees Kai, he pushes himself off his cot and calls out; Manu can't hear their conversation, but it sounds like they're arguing.

Another man has taken possession of an empty stretch of floor for his impressive martial arts practice, sweat luminous on his gold-white skin. He's bare chested and graceful, his glorious model's abs marred by a wicked-looking scar that traces the jut of his left hipbone before veering south below the waistband of his loose trousers.

There's a girl in the far corner. Mousy and small, she's picked a cot nearest the wall and is keeping to herself, absorbed in the glare of some type of hand terminal Manu's never seen before, glossy black hair falling in a curtain to obscure her face.

And there's the reason she's chosen that cot: a tall woman, a slice of muscle with blue-black skin and well-toned shoulders, prison tattoos stamped behind her ears and tracked down her inner arms. The women aren't talking, no sign to show they mean anything to each other except that the tall black woman looks up from her comm and gives him a glare when she catches him looking at the girl behind her.

There's a third cot on the near side of the black woman. Manu walks over.

"Manu Juric," he says, thrusting out a hand. She regards him coolly, then takes it. He expects a power play, but her grip is just firm.

"Gia."

The girl behind her doesn't look up. Gia ignores her, so Manu does, too.

"This cot taken?"

Gia shrugs, and he drops his jacket. The heavy denim hits the barely-there mattress with a sorry thud, and the space between Manu's shoulder blades twitches in anticipation.

"Man, what a job," he says, and gets nothing. "Be a trip, yeah?" It's poor bait and Gia doesn't stoop to it, just goes back to reading on her comm. "You been waiting around long?"

"You gonna keep talking all day?" Gia scrolls down without looking up.

"Probably not."

"Glad to hear it. Washroom's that way, you wanna clean yourself up."

The blood from the shallow cut has dried itchy on his cheek; he can feel it flaking as he gives Gia a smile she doesn't look up to see. Probably best to take care of it sooner rather than later.

"Thanks. Nice meeting you," he says, and gets no response.

He takes as long as he dares in the washroom. He looks like he spent the night chained to a chair in Willem Jaantzen's murder dungeon, and he decides it's not the most flattering look he's ever sported. He gingerly scrubs the blood off his cheek — though he can't get it out of his collar — and splashes cold water on his face. It'll have to do.

"Everybody round up," Kai's yelling as Manu comes back out.

With how many cots are in the warehouse, Manu expects "everybody" to be a few more than what it actually is. So far they are six: Gia, her little mouse, Kai, the martial arts model, the surly hook-nosed bruiser, and Manu.

Shitty team, is what he's thinking. He looks around to see what everyone else thinks. The answer is unclear.

The shitty team gathers around the desk. It's one of those cheap ones: disposable, self-destructive if things don't go well. Or if they do, and you just don't feel like hiring a crew to move it. Or if the power surges. Or somebody accidentally spills a cup of coffee down the circuitry.

Kai powers it on, thumps it with his fist when it blinks. It's showing a map. Manu's on the wrong side, but this city's an old friend. They're looking at the Tamarind District — there's that swanky bar his ex, Marisa, kept insisting they go to and he had to pay for.

"The job's this." Kai zooms in on the map, mumbling curses under his breath as the grainy hologram flickers, the graphics pulled kicking and screaming through the wiring of the cheap desk. The image finally snaps clear. "Smash and grab, more details on the target to come. But for now, know that what we need's here." The stubby finger points at an address across the street from the swanky bar. Manu recognizes the hotel, the Blue Falcon.

He lets out a low whistle. "Only Bulari's finest," he says, and Kai gives him a look.

The mousy girl has ended up beside him. She glances at him as though seeing him for the first time, then leans forward to see where Kai's pointing. "Where is that?"

"Posh hotel," Kai says. "Place's called the Blue Falcon." He glances at Manu. "You been there?"

"I never stayed there or anything, but yeah, I've been." To the lobby. During that night trying to get kicked out of bars with his buddies. They hadn't made it past the first set of doors.

"What's the target?" This from the martial arts model. Manu looks up, taking the chance to appreciate the man close up. He's rangy, with brassy, shaggy hair. He brushes it off chiseled cheekbones as he waits for Kai's answer.

"Details to come," Kai says. "It's a fast job. We're expecting a courier to pick up the goods. Our job is to intercept. Easy money."

"Famous last words," says the bruiser. Red-earth skin on this one, cracked through with years of too much sun and too many drugs. His black eyes hold challenge for Kai. "How do we know you've got our back?"

"Because I already gave you my word, Beni," a new voice says. Manu doesn't need to turn to look to see who it is.

Willem Jaantzen walks into the room. He's changed into a new suit since Manu saw him last, this one smoky gray. Manu didn't get any blood on Jaantzen's last suit, but he must've put a few bullet holes in it. Or maybe the man just likes a good costume change. Manu can appreciate that.

Jaantzen takes up a position at the head of the desk; Kai

steps to the side, but there's a moment's hesitation Jaantzen doesn't seem to notice. Manu's going to have to be careful not to get in between those two.

"Let's all get to know each other, shall we?" boss man says. "My name is Willem Jaantzen. I'll be running this operation."

"And who are you?" asks the bruiser Jaantzen called Beni.

Manu expects fury, from what he's heard of Jaantzen's temperament, but the man only hits Beni with a mild, evaluating look. Manu might even say it bordered on amusement. He glances around the table to see who else doesn't know who's hired them; sees only the white-gold man with a guarded look. The two women are staring at Beni like he's just said New Sarjun was flat. Kai looks . . . Kai just looks like Kai. Kinda murderous, kinda dumb.

"I'm the one who's running this operation," Jaantzen says again.

"And who are *you*, man?" Manu asks of Beni. He gets a look of distrust from the red-earth man, smiles back.

"Name's Beni Chav. You need to get somewhere quick, I'm your man."

"Mr. Chav is quite skilled," Jaantzen says. "He spent a decade racing Flat Creek, and a few more years on the pro circuit here in Bulari. I believe he has — and correct me if I'm wrong, Mr. Chav — two gold medals and three silvers. Very commendable, though not a complete surprise given his family's history on the track. He'd probably still be there now, save for certain money problems brought on by his penchant for gambling. Which might not have been a problem, except that his mother developed Matiz's syndrome, and his father had to start dealing in shard to pay her medical bills." Jaantzen fixes him with a stare. "Shall I go on."

Beni's nostrils flare, just a touch, and Manu can see the same thought in everyone's expressions: What does he know about me?

"I got this job through a contractor," Beni finally says. Grudging tone, slouching in his chair. Manu notes the way he tends to lean — to the left — and judges the shots he may need to take accordingly.

"Still, it pays to do a touch of research on the people you'll be working with," Jaantzen says mildly. He turns one hand out to the martial arts model, the other to Manu. "Oriol Sina, meet Manu Juric. You two have similar skill sets. You'll be working closely with Kai."

"And what exactly are the skill sets?" Gia's watching him with narrowed eyes.

"Ballroom dancing champions, us," says Manu. Across from him Oriol cracks a smile, the corners of his eyes crinkling. Manu wants to keep watching him forever — and not just because he's easy on the eyes. He's one of the most relaxed-looking humans Manu has ever come across. It's soothing.

"They're both excellent at killing people," Jaantzen says, holding Manu's gaze for the briefest of seconds. Mostly excellent, thinks Manu. Gia rolls her eyes. A stitch appears on the mousy girl's brow.

"You'll both especially want to play nice with Giaconda," Jaantzen says. "She'll be sewing you up if you get yourselves sliced open." He gives Manu a long look. "Particularly if you step on your partner's toes."

Manu ignores the jab, but doesn't try to hide his surprise at the rest. He'd taken Gia for a hired gun herself, with those lean, muscular arms and prison tattoos. "You're a doctor?"

"Gia coordinates," Jaantzen says simply. "When we're done here, let Gia know what you need."

Only one left unintroduced in this little crew. The mousy girl has been watching the proceedings with a look of wariness, a flutter of anxious knuckle cracks that only pause when she's watching Jaantzen. Manu notes that with interest. Something about the way she holds herself reminds him of someone, some ghost from the past he can't quite put a finger on. For a minute he thinks it's Marisa — that serious little downturn to the mouth — but that doesn't quite track.

"And what's she do?" Beni gets a second wind of gruffness and jabs a finger in the girl's direction like a dog that doesn't understand it's lost the fight. Good to know.

"Toshiyo will be our eyes in the sky," Jaantzen says. "She will be working closely with me. That means if you hear her give an order, you obey it instantly."

That little slip of a girl, giving orders? Manu can see the thought reflected on the faces of everyone around the table — even Gia. Toshiyo's hand creeps up to cover her throat.

"Understood," Manu says, tapping his fingers to his forehead in a quick salute to her. She gives him a faint smile, shoulders relaxing slightly. "What's our target?"

Jaantzen nods to him; it almost seems appreciative. "You're to retrieve something important. That's all you need to know for today." Manu barely holds back a snort; he's only been brought in for a couple group contract gigs, all back before he had enough of a rep that he could make a living on his own. They were always the same: We'll tell you what you need to know, when you need to know it. Like every mob boss had gone to the same crime leadership seminar.

"We'll spend tomorrow gathering supplies, so tell Gia what you need," Jaantzen says. "I'll speak with you all then."

And with that the big boss man tugs a cuff into place and walks out the door.

The shitty team stays, staring at the grainy hologram — and at each other — with suspicion.

This is going to be terrible.

4

HOW TO MAKE FRIENDS

Time to make the rounds.

Manu decides to start with the model martial artist, on account of if he's going to get shot down, it might as well be by the prettiest face in the room.

Oriol's sitting on his cot alone, brassy hair falling into his eyes as he types something into his comm. Wiry tendons dance in his forearms as his fingers move; when he sees Manu approaching he slips the device into his duffel.

"What's your deal, man?" Oriol says, but it's curiosity, not a challenge. He leans back on his elbows, feet crossed at the ankles. He's still barefoot.

Manu sits on the cot across from him, trying self-consciously to match Oriol's casual pose. "My deal?"

"You an assassin? Hired gun? What's your deal."

"Bounty hunter, these days."

The look on Oriol's face, that raised eyebrow and a smirk.

"Bounty hunter." Manu waits for commentary; it doesn't come.

"How about you?" Manu asks.

"My deal is I don't like to talk about myself," Oriol says. But the way he holds himself says enough. That faint hint of an Indiran accent — New Manila, maybe — the reflexes and the moves he was showing off earlier. Oriol's been well trained, and Manu'll be damned if it wasn't by the Indiran Alliance. Manu wonders what's got an ex-soldier doing crime on the wrong planet these days.

An uneasy feeling pokes at the back of Manu's mind. Whatever the job is, this crew is too odd a mix. He'd expected thugs like Beni and Kai to be running with Jaantzen, and Gia with her prison tats isn't a stretch. But Oriol seems too sophisticated for this kind of mess. And the girl, Toshiyo . . . He wonders if she's been kidnapped, somehow. Brainwashed.

"Job seems rushed, yeah?" he asks. "What's your take?"

"I don't have one."

"Not into speculation?"

"I get the job done, then get out."

"You're not the type likes to draw out the fun? I'll keep that in mind."

Oriol shoots him a wry look. "I take the money that's offered."

"I'll keep that in mind, too," Manu says with a wink.

The response he gets is a raised brow.

"You worked with the man before?"

It's the subtle kick of his foot that tells Manu no, though Oriol only shrugs.

"How'd you get the gig?"

"Man, anybody tell you you ask too many questions?"

"Just Gia so far today. Oh, and Kai."

Oriol's gaze slides to the cut on Manu's cheek. His expression is dark, but it's gone so quickly most would've missed it. No love lost between Kai and Oriol, then. Good to know.

"Well. Manu Juric, you ask too many questions," Oriol says. "Another man might tell you that with his fist."

Manu knows who those other men are — he was raised by one — and he knew Oriol wasn't one of them when he started his pestering. But Oriol just lays back on the cot, one knee bent, eyes closed, one arm folded under his head. His shirt's riding up just enough for Manu to get another glimpse of the jagged scar scrawled over his hipbone.

Gia catches his eye from across the room; she's typing into a hand terminal, one hip cocked against the desk, Kai at her side. She jerks her chin, a summons.

"I'm gonna go talk to Gia. You got everything you need?"

Oriol doesn't open his eyes. "I'll talk to Gia myself," he says.

———

Kai pulls himself taller as Manu walks up; if Gia notices the display, she's ignoring it. Manu gives the big man his deference in a quick nod — his pride has never been dependent on pissing contests. Kai's chin lifts in satisfaction.

"Everything I need's in my gear bag," Manu says, and Gia looks up from her comm. "But I could probably use some more of those hornet tags."

Gia arches an eyebrow. "What for?"

"They're distracting. And fun."

"Nobody's blowing up anything," Kai growls.

Manu shrugs. "You got it, boss. Then I just need a change of clothes."

Gia's gaze flickers to the blood soaking into his collar before she gives him a once-over. "I think my sister's got pants in her closet would fit you. Want me to pick up some eyeliner from her, too?"

Manu flashes his teeth in a smile. "Nah, I got some in my gear bag. Along with several guns I think you'll find quite impressive."

She's giving him a look, chin down and eyebrows raised like is he for real.

"Several," he says again, and now he can see Gia can't decide whether to laugh or tell him to fuck off. They're making baby steps.

Kai's just giving him a glare — the big man's standard expression, Manu's starting to think. He wonders if the glare softens when he's kissing a lover. Or being snuggled by puppies. Manu wonders what it would take to make Kai laugh.

"You *are* gonna give me my gear bag back, yeah?" he asks the big man, gets a reluctant nod. "And my comm? Good." Turns back to Gia. "Then I just need the change of clothes. Thanks, Giaconda." A flare of nostrils. Ah, noted. That's not the name to use in the future.

"Gia, I sent a list to your comm," says a voice from behind him; Manu lifts his chin to greet the mousy girl. Toshiyo. She blinks at him, like she's trying to remember where she's seen him before.

"How did you know my — " Gia's comm buzzes. She frowns at it. "What's a Lumar lens?"

Toshiyo launches into an explanation while Gia scrambles to take notes.

Manu tunes it out, more amused by watching Kai try to follow along. "What's our objective?" Manu asks him.

The big man blinks. "Ain't important."

"I'd say it's pretty important, if it's worth whatever you're paying us all," he says, and he hears Toshiyo's explanation stutter and loop, just the once; she's listening. Gia's stylus is paused over her comm, but she's still got her eyes on Toshiyo. "I'm sure we didn't all come out of the bargain basement like yours truly."

A muscle's twitching in Kai's jaw. "Ain't important," he says again, and Gia starts typing along with Toshiyo's explanation once more.

"Thanks, boss," Manu says with a smile so wide it stings his cheek.

As he turns to go, Kai grunts something; Manu turns back in time to catch the object Kai's tossed to him.

His comm.

There's that, at least.

It's nice to have his comm back, but Manu'd really kill for his gear bag right about now. Not for the weaponry — Manu isn't stupid enough to give that a try, not until he knows the lay of the land. But he has a toothbrush in there, a change of underwear. The basics.

And some not-so-basics: a tiny bottle of good face wash, eyeliner, deodorant. He won't try to get the word from Oriol again today, but Manu still smells like old blood and fear-sweat from the murder dungeon and he's certain it'll be wafting over to Gia and Toshiyo tonight. Sorry, ladies.

Still, the comm is something. He thumbs it on, is gratified to see that they haven't managed to break his encryption, though they've obviously tried.

A single message is buried in his secret inbox, from Sylla's number, from hours earlier: CALL ME.

Manu lies back on his cot and gives the screen a few taps. CANT TALK NOW JOBS STILL ON.

He waits. Fifteen seconds, maybe twenty before his screen flashes.

SO YOUR STILL ALIVE. CALL ME.

CANT TALK NOW.

CALL ME.

Manu sits half-up on his cot. Kai and Beni are arguing in the corner, Oriol appears to be trying to sleep, Gia is cleaning a gun — Manu'll have to watch where she stashes that, it could be his chance — and Toshiyo is back on her cot exactly as he first saw her, hunched over her strange hand terminal behind a curtain of silky black hair.

There's a door across from the washroom that leads to a balcony. Manu strolls towards it, and except for a brief glance from Kai no one goes after him. Good to know: Kai doesn't think there's any escape this way.

Kai's right. It's just a narrow overhang overlooking nothing but other warehouses, with a long and messy fall to the pavement below. They're not far from the docking yards, and the rumble of magtrucks on the shipping lanes is loud and close. If they're bugging conversations out here they probably can't pick up much.

Manu taps out Sylla's number. Leans back against the low wall surrounding the balcony so he can see the door, the sharp edge of the concrete biting into his lower back. His cheek feels swollen and fever hot in the cool night air; it aches to put on the fake smile he affects even though he's only initiated a voice call.

Sylla's fast to answer. "Manu. Hon." Her husky voice is two ragged steps past sultry, but she still wields it like a diva. "Thank God."

The sentiment's feigned, he knows, but it still hooks him sharp right below the sternum. When's the last time he came through a bad job and had someone care he'd made it? Not since Marisa — well, not since before he told her what he actually did for a living.

Although even in the good days, Marisa had really only cared that he'd made it to dinner on time.

"I'm all good," he says, half to Sylla, half to himself. "I'm fine."

"I was so worried about you."

"No need to worry." But Manu spikes to attention. Sylla doesn't worry about full crew, much less a loner like him. And as much as he'd like to flatter himself, she's not that interested in anything but his potential as a crew member.

And if she's not worried about him, that means she's worried about what he might say to Jaantzen.

"Coulda got yourself hurt," Sylla purrs.

"Nobody knows a thing," he says, hoping that's enough to reassure her.

"Mmm?" Muffled, she's talking to someone away from the mic. There's a familiar noise in the background, something he can't quite place, like a wind chime. He tries to remember if Sylla has any wind chimes in her lair.

"Nobody here knows about us."

"Of course not. Where are you, hon?"

"I'm still on the job. I'm safe." Not that he believes that. But she needs to, or she'll think he's a liability.

He hears that muffled voice again, wonders if they're trying to track him. That should be impossible with this comm, but still he won't bet his life on it. That familiar chiming comes again from the other end of the line, along with a sound like a magtruck shuddering on a patch of bent track. He frowns. He doesn't think Sylla's lair is on a magtruck line.

"You going back to your place?" she asks.

"I'm still on the job."

Sharp sucked-in breath, a snip of clicking teeth. "You with him?"

"Undercover, like."

She snaps a command to whoever's out of range of the comm. "Like hell, undercover. I heard about the circus you put on at his bar — word's been spreading thick, Manu. Old folks' homes is buzzing with the news. Babies talkin bout it, hon. You think you're undercover with him, you being played." A wet cough. "And you being played, *I* being played."

"Don't worry about it. It's under control."

"Don't worry? I don't just have your sorry ass to take care

of. Hon, I got me a whole crew I gotta keep safe. Come on in. I'll protect you."

But he's not crew, and he never will be after this botched attempt. Not unless he can make amends, pass the attack at the bar off as Phase One of the Flashy Secret Plan. Sylla wants him to come in, but not so she can protect him. She wants to protect her own.

And Manu isn't one of her own.

"Manu? Hon? You there?"

Manu's been listening to the silence beyond her voice. He knows that familiar shuddering magtruck catching on the bent track. He knows that wind chime.

Marisa bought it for him for his birthday last year.

Sylla Mar and her thugs are inside his apartment.

"Manu?"

"I'm still on the job," is all he says. "Trust me."

He thumbs off the call.

Sylla's hunting him already.

He rubs the back of his neck and stares at the bright maw of doorway he just came through. It dawns on him that the safest place for him to be right now is inside that warehouse working for Bulari's most hated thug.

He comes back to Sylla without this kill, he's a dead man.

5

EASY PEASY

When he comes back in, everyone's as he left them. Beni and Kai both look up as he enters; Gia's with them now, too, and someone's pulled out a pack of holocards. The three are playing a surly game of mystix; Beni plucks a card from the table and barks out profanity as it shifts from red to green and spoils the flush he thought he'd drawn.

Toshiyo's still sitting crosslegged on her cot, attention buried in her hand terminal.

Manu drags his feet as he approaches, scuffs his heel. Coughs. Toshiyo doesn't seem to track his approach. "Hey," he says when he's standing at the foot of her cot.

Toshiyo jumps, startled. She blinks at him a moment as though placing him. "Manu," she says, and he's not sure if it's a greeting or she's just jogging her own memory.

"Yeah, hey." He jerks his chin over his shoulder at the card game. "Not much for mystix?"

Toshiyo blinks over at the others. "What are they playing?"

"Seriously? Where you from?"

"Korin. Ruby Basin. I don't play a lot of games."

"Everybody here's playing some sort of game." He tries to say it lightly, like it doesn't mean anything.

"I'm not playing a game," Toshiyo says, tilting her hand terminal towards him. Misunderstanding. "I'm getting into the security feeds at the hotel."

"Yeah? Anything good?" She's scooted over on her cot, so he sits, assuming it's an invitation. She doesn't seem to notice.

"They have three video systems," Toshiyo says. "I've only gotten into the first one." Her hand terminal's screen is a sandstorm of letters and numbers; Manu can't make heads or tails of it. "This is the main feed — it looks like it covers most of the hotel, except for the lobby. The two other feeds cover various parts of the floor, but they're a lot harder to break into."

"Lemme guess. We need eyes in the lobby."

"It's not fun without a challenge."

Manu glances at her, but the girl doesn't seem to be saying it ironically. "You try saying that when you're the one might have to walk in and shoot up the place," he says.

Toshiyo blinks at him as though considering if she'd miss him. Or any of them. "What happened to your face?" she asks instead.

"It's a new part of my beauty regimen," Manu says. "Do you think it's working?"

Toshiyo just laughs. "I bet Gia could fix it up quick so it doesn't scar," she says. "I've seen a lot of that in the mines —

medtech is expensive out there, but plenty of people are willing to pay if it's their face."

"I'll ask her about that," Manu says, but he won't — not until after. Until this job's done, he's got a reminder every time he looks in the mirror. Thing is, Manu's still not sure what he wants the cut to remind him of. That he screwed up bad, or that he owes Kai a scar of his own. A bit of both, he guesses.

"What's your deal?" he asks.

"My deal?" Toshiyo frowns at him. "Oh — I analyze data for Blacklode. Analyzed, I mean. I'm a — was an ops tech."

"How do you get in with this crew? It's an awful long way from Ko — from the Ruby Basin." He already can't remember the name of the shit little town she just said she was from.

"Oh." Toshiyo blushes, stares down at the device in her hands. "Jaantzen paid off my indenture."

"He bought out your indenture?" But that isn't what she said, is it. Manu's eyes go wide. "He *paid off* your indenture? Like, just so you'd do this job?"

"I don't think I'm supposed to talk about it," Toshiyo says, wincing, and for a split second Manu feels guilt at pressing her so far — but that's the game, isn't it? Get the information? He's not on anyone's side here.

"I tried to collect a bounty on Jaantzen," he says. Change the subject, give her some quid pro quo to make her comfortable again. "But I guess I managed to both underestimate him and impress him at the same time. He convinced me to join his crew instead." None of the crew seem the type to gossip, but if Toshiyo isn't tight with her stories — and she's clearly not — this is the version he'd rather get around. None of this

"He tied me to a chair and Kai beat me to a bloody pulp" nonsense.

"He's a very impressive man," Toshiyo says, then presses her lips tight. He's spooked her, now.

The gesture seems familiar — and Manu finally places it. Toshiyo's got a way about her that reminds him of a cousin, years ago.

His only cousin, she was about his age. He remembers years of rambunctious laughter getting shushed in their grandmother's house, how those years faded just like her color as she and Manu got older and both their daddies got meaner. Siggy, everybody called her. Sigmaria was her real name, just like that Arquellian pop star who was making the rounds on the music feeds at the time.

What happened to cousin Siggy, he remembers being told by his father with a backhand, by his grandmother with a pinch to the arm, was none of his business. None of his business that Siggy stopped speaking, stopped playing, turned gray and frozen when her own father came back to their grandmother's to pick her up each night.

Just like whatever happens to Toshiyo or Oriol or Sylla or whoever is none of his business.

Manu's not on anyone's team but his own.

"Hey, you got a map of the area around that hotel? There's this bar, right across the street. My old boyfriend used to love that place." It had actually been Marisa's favorite, but Toshiyo sits up straighter, and whether it's the distraction of the work or the assumption that he won't be hitting on her, he's not sure. Whatever it is, she snaps back into herself.

"Yeah, I got that right here." Again, Manu can only see streams of numbers on her hand terminal. "I'll send that over."

She's easy peasy, which is good. If Toshiyo is working close with Jaantzen, being tight with her might just be his key to getting close to his target without arousing suspicion. Because Jaantzen certainly isn't going to let him into killing distance on his own.

"Great. My number is — " His comm's screen flashes. Manu frowns at it. "How'd you get this number?"

Toshiyo's eyebrows knit together like the question doesn't make sense. He thinks of the attempted break-in on his comm.

"Did you try to get through my comm's encryptions earlier?"

"No, do you need me to? It's easy." No guile in that face. He's suddenly absurdly grateful that Kai hadn't thought to ask her.

"Nah, I'm good. Thanks for the map." He stands, holds out a hand that Toshiyo doesn't notice; she's gone back to her terminal.

He frowns down at her. The curve of her neck looks just like Siggy, and it gives him a queasy sense of guilt he can't quite quell. "Hey, Tosh. A bit of advice," he says, forgetting the game for a moment. She looks up, blinks. "You can't trust any of us."

"I don't," Toshiyo says defensively. "I mean, not the others. But . . ."

"But I seem nice." She nods, and Manu gives her his best smile, brushing off the tiniest part of him that feels like shit. "Being friendly's just the way I get what I want. But you gotta have just as much of a guard up for friendly as you do for mean."

"Sorry," Toshiyo says.

Manu laughs. "You and me don't have no debt with each other, but ain't everybody here's on the same side."

Toshiyo frowns at him. "But aren't we all working for Jaantzen?"

"I hope so."

Toshiyo just squints back down at her terminal, but Manu looks up to see Gia watching him, unfriendly. He feels Gia's eyes on him the whole time he saunters to the washroom. Like she knows what he's thinking. He winks at her, shuts the door behind him. Gonna be a long night, he thinks, baring his teeth to the mirror and rubbing them half-clean with the meat of his index finger.

Gonna be a long night.

6

FUN AT THE TERMINAL

Morning.

Manu wakes coughing from a dream of thick cigar smoke to a smothering cloud of fabric over his face. He claws at it, gasping, and finds pants. Shirts.

Across the room, Beni and Oriol are laughing over mugs of coffee. Gia's standing at the foot of his cot with a faint smile. A pecking order is clearly being established.

Manu takes a deep breath.

He doesn't care about pecking orders. They just keep you from noticing who you should really be paying attention to.

He examines the garments to find mediocre fabrics, modern styles. Boring colors: grays and blues. "Looks like they'll fit," he says. He swings his legs over the side of his cot, makes no note he's annoyed.

His foot hits something familiar — his gear bag. He

unseals it and paws through the contents. No weapons, what a surprise, but the rest of his stuff is there. It'll do.

Manu locks himself in the washroom and checks his comm, but there's no message from Sylla. No message from his landlady, either, so maybe Sylla hasn't yet torched his apartment in anger. That's a good sign.

For a fraction of a second he thinks of messaging Sylla to see if she'll water his jadau plant, but the impulse towards self-destruction flames out as soon as it strikes. Don't push her buttons, Manu. Don't make her think you're joking about this job.

Don't let on you know how serious the stakes are.

He can't get the cloying reek of cigar smoke out of his nostrils, and he sniffs at the clothes Gia brought him to see if it's something there or if it's just a trick of the brain, lingering from his dream.

He knows the smoke — it's his grandma's, the brand she used to smoke during the long hours of his childhood he spent under her care. The brand's old-fashioned, but he still catches whiffs of it sometimes and is transported back to her house in an instant, heart dropped out of his chest like he's nine again and he and Siggy are tiptoeing through that magical wonderland their grandmother called home.

He remembers it as a maze: every garment Grandma ever owned folded neatly in teetering piles when her closet became too full; the packaging materials for every item she might want to return someday shoved in the corner, though those items had worn out years before; dusty glass bottles stacked in crates to exchange at a corner store long gone out of business.

It was stuffed with the fascinating odds and ends she'd

brought home, no rhyme or reason but that she might need them someday. She had seven brooms, three electric tea kettles, fourteen obsolete comms. A complete set of a child's novelty luggage printed with tourist scenes from Indira and slapped with slogans: Visit the Green Planet. No place to sit.

He understood now that she'd been future-proofing her life, clinging to anything and everything she might need, clinging to her sons and her grandchildren with a death grip. And the same blind eye that meant she couldn't be convinced to throw out the coat with the torn-off sleeve meant she couldn't see what her sons were doing to her grandchildren, no matter how Siggy started to vanish and Manu to go surly.

She couldn't choose between two broke-down armchairs, let alone choose between her drunk-ass sons and her crimeless grandchildren.

Manu's not a hoarder — not of things, not of people.

You can't keep hold of anybody. He'd learned that trying to keep hold of Siggy. Trying to keep hold of Marisa. People won't choose you, so why bother choosing them?

He washes up in the sink, brushes his teeth, changes into the new clothes. Reapplies his eyeliner, adding a streak of cobalt blue along the upper lash line just to annoy Gia.

Grins into the mirror until the cut on his cheek cracks faintly.

Everything about this job feels like a death trap — including the memories it's dredging up.

Let's get this done and get out.

Gia waves him over as he drops his bag on his cot. "You'll come with me to pick up the gear," she says.

Across the room, Beni and Oriol are conferring with Toshiyo. "What're they up to?" Manu says.

"Reconnaissance. Toshiyo's hacked the hotel's main security feeds, but there's a secondary system she hasn't been able to patch into. Needs a man on the ground. C'mere. Let me fix that cheek."

"Maybe later."

Way she's watching him, Manu wonders if she knows where he got it. Wonders if she's in with Kai. Wonders if she got the same threats from Kai and Jaantzen to get her cooperation, or if she joined up willing and able.

For a moment there's a hesitation in her expression that borders on genuine compassion, but the moment vanishes. "Yeah, I ain't walking around the terminal with you looking like that. Come here."

And he finds himself sitting on her cot while she rummages through her gear. A cool smear of knitting gel, and he can feel the local anesthetic kicking in to numb the sting as the gel dissolves the scabs. Gia swabs his jawline to catch a rolling bead of new blood.

"You grew up in Bulari, yeah?" she asks.

"You tell that by the accent, or my charming disposition?"

"I can tell by how full you are of yourself. Just like every Bulari boy I ever met."

"Glad I live up to expectations."

Gia ignores him and pulls a device the size of her thumb out of her bag. She twists it and the end glows blue; it's soothingly warm when she presses it against the cut. His cheek begins to itch. It's maddening.

"How good a surgeon are you?" Manu asks.

Gia's fingers are strong and sure, holding his jaw. "Stop talking, Manu."

"Like, you can reattach nerves with your eyes closed? Or mostly battle-trained?"

Battle-trained is his working theory. She's got a tattoo in the crook of the elbow: two bars across a half circle looks like a setting sun. Redrock Prison. It's the prison the Indiran Alliance has north of the impassable Jupari Desert belt, where they mostly take terrorists and other riffraff they capture off-planet and don't want to ship all the way home to Indira. They got the concession from New Sarjun a century ago somehow, and no amount of fuss these days will make them give it back.

Tattoo like that from Redrock, this Giaconda probably fought in an anti-Alliance skirmish or two. Some slum kid like himself, radicalized against the man.

But:

"I trained at Sulila," Gia says, like it's nothing. She tilts his head with her fingers, examining her work. "I've never tried to reattach nerves with my eyes closed, but given how many times I've done it with my eyes open, I'd trust me blindfolded over most anybody else you could find."

Manu lets himself look impressed — it isn't hard, and Gia deserves it.

Sulila is ridiculously elite and hardcore religious — though the latter is nothing he's sensing off Gia. There aren't many who can afford to pay for Sulila Corp.'s medical school on their own, and it's expensive enough that few of their graduates ever earn out their indentures. Whoever bought Gia's could still be looking for her, time spent in Redrock or no.

At least once a day, Manu finds himself grateful that he dropped out of Hypatia's Carama Town school and started working for his dad the bookie. God only knows what kind of trouble he'd be in if he'd gotten himself an indenture.

"I suppose you'll do in a pinch," he jokes, and Gia only raises an eyebrow and begins to swab off the wound.

"The scar's still visible, but it should heal up to nothing so long as you stay out of the sun and stop pissing people off," Gia says, stepping back to look at him critically. "Though that seems like a long shot. You need to work on your game with the ladies."

"My game with the ladies is just fine," Manu says.

"Well then I just ain't your type."

He shoots her a glance. "What, you don't like guys?"

"I'm not gullible."

"You just ain't learned to like me yet."

Gia pulls her comm out of her pocket, starts typing something in. "Just a sec," she says. "Gotta make a note to pick up an extra case of bandages. Might need it, you keep annoying me."

Manu kicks back and stretches his arms up high overhead; he catches her quick glance at his abs before she turns away.

"Worthwhile investment," he says.

———

Geordi Jimenez Terminal is in a fairly seedy part of town,

near the warehouses and the shipping yards. Manu hasn't spent much time here, apart from the occasional need to get a specialty weapon or two. In fact, the last time he was here was to pick up the gear he used to tear up the Bronze Room.

Those had been fun.

"You know what this plan is missing," he says. "Explosives. We can still get me a dozen of those hornet tags. I know a guy."

Gia gives him side-eye. "You know what I really hate doing?" she asks. "Fixing up people who've been exploded."

"I've never gotten myself exploded."

"Yeah? In my experience, most idiots haven't until it happens to them." She steers him around a drunk passed out in the stairwell.

"What are we picking up, if not explosives?" Manu asks, acting incredulous.

Gia shoots him a look. "There are so many other things," she says. "Besides explosives. Neural stunners, for example. Simple. Effective. Don't require a lot of cleanup on the doctor's end."

"Neural stunners don't make a loud bang."

"Stealth. Look it up."

"Neural stunners are boring."

Gia rolls her eyes. "Sometimes boring is a blessing, kid."

They've gone down to level C, and it's like a carnival down here: loud and echoey, the sounds of laughter, slamming doors, shouted curses pinging off the high metal walls and cavernous ceiling. Gia says something he can't hear. Manu leans towards her. "What?" he shouts.

"I said it's all the way at the end," she shouts back.

He follows her, threading through the throngs of people. It's the middle of the day, which is one of the better times to do business in level C of the terminal. Get out of the heat and the dust of Bulari's midday scorchers, get underground where it's naturally cool.

And, at midday, the lunch stands are running at full speed. Sizzling fat and clinking silverware, the shouts of vendors hawking fried noodles, samosas, anticuchos. Manu's stomach grumbles. There's nothing to eat at the warehouse but a pile of military-grade ration packs and coffee substitute with no sugar. Maybe they'll have time to sample the food carts afterwards.

Their destination is almost all the way to the end of the terminal, where you find the businesses that don't rely on foot traffic. It's quieter here, the crowd orbiting mainly around the food carts and other services near the entrance.

Here are the shipping companies, the small cargo brokers, the salvage ops who don't need a more visible spot in the terminal because their commerce comes from word of mouth spread through Bulari's underbelly. Most of the stalls at this end are shuttered, metal grates rolled down and locked.

Gia's checking numbers on the stalls; she pauses in front of C-746. It's shuttered, but she knocks on the grate. The silence goes on for too long.

"We got the right time, yeah?"

Gia nods, but doesn't answer. She's tense, fingers itching towards the holster on her hip. Manu checks his own weapons — she gave him a pair of pistols once they were on the road — then scans the room around them. Yawns.

"Who are these guys?" He hadn't bothered asking earlier;

he didn't think she would tell him. But now he can scent her nerves and it's put her off-balance. Opened up just the slightest chink in her armor against him. It's times like these when people find him helpful.

"Contacts I was given."

Given. That explains some of her unease. "By Jaantzen?"

"You ask a lot of questions."

"I get that a lot," Manu says.

A metal *snick* sounds from the other side of the grate, and the door rolls up with a clatter.

There's three people inside. The one who rolled up the grate, and two others, a man and a woman, both casually armed with vicious-looking pulse carbines. Manu smiles and opens his hands, nonthreatening. Gia lifts her chin at them in greeting.

"Good morning," she says. "I trust the weapons aren't necessary."

The man who rolled up the grate just shrugs. He's scrawny, shaved head, metallic-ink tattoos winding around his wrists. "We ain't met you before. Ain't gonna take chances."

"We're not here to make trouble," Gia says. "We already gave you half the money. Soon as we see the goods, the other half is yours."

The man purses his lips over his shoulder. "Goods are over there."

The other two stand back to let them pass back into the stall. Back into a death trap, Manu thinks.

He glances at Gia; she's thinking the same thing. "I'd like to take a look at it here in the light, if you don't mind."

She wins the staring match. The two thugs put down their

weapons and bring forward a crate, set it near the entrance to the stall.

The tattooed man leans forward to type a code into the lock, and the top of the crate slides open. Manu stands back to cover Gia while she checks the contents. She pulls out two empty duffel bags, roots through the rest. "It looks like it's all here."

"Of course it is," the tattooed man says.

While Manu keeps an eye on the thugs, Gia piles the contents of the crates into the two duffels. She pulls out her comm. "I'm having the money transferred."

The tattooed man nods, waiting. A soft chime; he pulls out his own comm. "I see it."

"So we're good, then," Gia says. She hands one of the duffels to Manu. Easy way she lifted it, he wasn't prepared for just how heavy it is. He shoulders it with a huff. Tattoos gives him a smirk; Manu ignores it. Let them think he's weak. More opportunities that way.

He shifts the duffel so his hands are free and the weight is good.

"Of course," Tattoos says. "Wouldn't wanna hold you up. I hear you got plans."

Gia stills. "What kind of plans have you heard about?"

Tattoos breaks into a long, slow grin. "Hear you got plans with the queen bee."

The queen bee?

"I haven't heard anything about that," Gia says, dismissive, and it's so casual Manu can't tell if she's lying.

Tattoos just raises an eyebrow. "No worries. May fortune smile on you," he says, and even before he's finished the sentence Gia's dropped her duffel and has him in a headlock, a pistol digging into his temple.

Manu and the two hired guns are slower to move, but he's quicker than them both and has his pistols out and pointed before they've quite caught on.

"Gia," Manu says.

"What the fuck's your problem?" Tattoos gasps.

"Why did you say that?" Gia asks, pistol digging harder. Tattoos puts his hands up. The hired guns have their attention on Manu's weapons. This is not going well.

"Gia," Manu says again. "What is this?"

"I want to know why he said that."

"Just a saying." Sweat is beading up on Tattoos' scalp; a trickle runs down his nose and splashes onto the concrete. "Just a thing you say, someone you know's going into battle."

A beat, then Gia slams her pistol back into its holster, lets Tattoos rise. But she keeps hold of his wrist, pushes his sleeve up to see his forearm.

One of the tattoos glimmers with microscopic opalescent beads embedded in the ink. The bulk of the image is clinging strands of red-blossomed devilweed, drawn so that the thorns seem to pierce his arm and draw blood. Three symbols are scrawled there in among the vines — Manu doesn't recognize them.

"'Money, beauty, death,'" says Gia. She lets go, shoulders her duffel bag again. "Come on," she says to Manu.

He covers her until she's out of the storage unit, then takes a few steps back himself. Tattoos seems mad, yeah, but mostly just confused. He doesn't look like he's about to kill them.

Manu hopes.

53

He's been wrong more than once this week.

"Sorry about all that, folks," he says. "Definitely owe you a drink next time."

"Get out," Tattoos spits, and Manu gives him a rueful smile, holsters his right pistol, keeps the dominant left ready to go.

But Tattoos just slams down the rolling door. Manu breathes a sigh of relief. He's sweating now, the scent sharp and raw.

Gia's on the move.

"What the fuck was that?" Manu says when he catches up with her. The way Gia is walking, heads are raising in Manu's peripheral vision, jackals scenting adrenaline on the wind. Manu grabs her arm. "You're calling attention," he says, and she glances at him. Slows.

"Sendera Dathúil," Gia says, like he should know what that means.

"What?"

"Dathúil," she repeats, like maybe he just hadn't heard her.

"And what the hell are they?"

"Redrock gang." She's walking fast again. Manu catches her arm and forces her back into the moment. "Started in Redrock, at least. Religious nuts. Believe some crazy shit about the end times."

"And they run weapons, too."

"Apparently."

Manu doesn't know what Jaantzen's getting them into, but he doesn't care. Right now, they just need to get out of here with the gear, and without a firefight. Gia's walking calmer, now, and everyone's ignoring them. The Sendera-whoever idiots aren't following them, but he can't know if they've called ahead, so he's scanning the room for anything he can find. For any body language out of place.

He's scanning, and he sees a lone woman taking her lunch at a noodle counter, twirling her ramen daintily with a fussy gesture Manu recognizes even before he sees her face.

He whirls, pivoting on his heel to dive deeper in the crowd, but it's already too late. Those wide, fox-brown eyes meet his in surprise, and she's fumbling for her comm, sloshing noodles over the bar in her hurry.

Jaxie, Sylla Mar's third in command.

Manu's melted into the crowd, but Jaxie spotted him for sure.

This is shaping up into a bad day.

7

PICKUP LINES

B ack at the ranch, Gia stops the spinner but doesn't move to get out. Manu gives her a look. The sharp line of her jaw is tense, a cord of muscle taut under her midnight skin. "We getting our stories straight first?" he asks when she doesn't seem ready to say anything.

Gia gives him a long, slow look. "Let me say my piece about Sendera Dathúil. I'm the one's got a problem with them. You just stay out of it."

"If they're so bad, why haven't I heard about them?"

Gia's quiet a minute. "You have," she says. It's a long time before she speaks again, but Manu waits.

"You know that ambassador's kid that got kidnapped last spring?" she asks. "That was them."

Manu raises an eyebrow. Of course he'd heard about that — everyone had. The kidnappers had taken the ransom, but still nobody'd found the kid.

57

"You think Jaantzen knew who they were when he set you up with them?"

He's using "you" deliberately, pushing her buttons. Trying to gauge the depth of her loyalty to Jaantzen. Toshiyo is clearly on the man's team, Beni and Oriol are clearly in it for the cash. Kai's in it for the power, but Manu can't figure out why Gia's here. She's putting on that mercenary vibe, same as Beni and Oriol, but there's something in the way she watches Jaantzen when he's in the room that makes Manu wonder if she doesn't owe him something deeper than work for hire.

Maybe she's got a debt to pay off, just like Manu.

"You think he knew you had a problem with them?"

But she only holds out a hand for his pistols. "I'm not here to think," Gia says, sharp and angry. And just like that her armor's back on.

Armor's on, but the way she slams the spinner into its dock shows he's hit a nerve. Some core of trust she used to have with Jaantzen has been broken.

A deep one, too, by the way her anger's got her seeing short, her attention only on what's in front of her nose — and what's raging in her mind.

Isn't that just perfect.

Gia's got her back to him for only a second, but it's all Manu needs to slip his hand inside the bag and grab a knife. He sticks it sheath and all down the back of his pants and shrugs his jacket into place before Gia turns around again.

The handle's awkward, digging painfully into his spine, but he doesn't care. He has a weapon.

It's all part of his brilliant plan:

Step One: Find a weapon.

Step Two: Find a way to be alone with Willem Jaantzen.

Step Three: Kill Jaantzen, earning the wrath of the very dangerous people involved with this job.

Step Four: Head home to Sylla Mar, who might be so angry she kills him anyway.

Step Five: Fame and glory.

Or something like that.

Manu shoulders the bag and leads the way towards the door, feeling Gia fall into step behind him. Killing Jaantzen was a terrible idea when Sylla suggested it to him, and it's an even more terrible idea now.

Manu has a sinking feeling about his plan.

But at least he has a knife.

———

Inside the warehouse, Toshiyo's sitting in front of one of her monitors; she glances in their general direction as Manu and Gia enter, but doesn't acknowledge them. "That's it," she says. "To the left."

Willem Jaantzen is there, arms crossed, standing over her shoulder. If one of the most notorious criminals in Bulari had been standing over his shoulder like that, Manu would have been jumpy as hell, but Toshiyo's relaxed. Or just absorbed in her work.

Jaantzen glances over at Manu and Gia. "Success?" he asks.

"All good," Manu answers. He sets his duffel on the table and stands back as Kai shoulders in to look things over.

"No, to the left," Toshiyo says.

JESSIE KWAK

She and Jaantzen are watching a POV camera on one monitor — it must be Oriol, judging by the ritzy interior of the Blue Falcon's lobby. On the second monitor, a shaky feed is jostling as Oriol adjusts a miniature camera. On the side of the screen, four of the six camera angles are already turned on, showing them nearly everything that Toshiyo hadn't been able to hack into.

"Right there," Toshiyo says, and Oriol clicks his tongue against the roof of his mouth twice in acknowledgement. The feed on the second monitor stills as Oriol adheres the miniature camera into place. Toshiyo leans in to study the feed. "Perfect," she says. She taps a button and the newest feed fills the fifth slot on the side of the screen.

"Last one is the entrance cam," Toshiyo says. "I need you to position it — right, you see that girl with the purple hair?" Two clicks. "Put the camera under the bartop, just below her elbow."

"I hope you've been practicing your pickup lines, Mr. Sina," Jaantzen says, and Oriol just sighs.

Manu grins. This oughta be good.

Jaantzen turns, mutes his mic. "And did everything go as planned on your end, Mr. Juric?"

On Oriol's POV feed, the purple-haired woman's face fills the monitor. She looks up, annoyed. Oriol's off to a good start.

"No problems," Manu says. Depending on your definition of problem, at least — they got away squeaky clean, though who can tell what will come down the pipeline as a result of Gia's little altercation and Jaxie spotting him.

Doesn't matter. The knife digs into his back as he shifts. "Got the goods, hit the road."

60

"What was your estimation of our contacts?" Jaantzen asks.

Is this a trap? Manu's working it through. Does Jaantzen know the men were Sendera Dathúil? Would he have cared? Probably not — he's got a reputation for using the worst and darkest crews.

Anyway, who Jaantzen uses for supply is not his problem. His problem is getting out of here alive and without getting on the shit list of every powerful person in Bulari: Jaantzen, Sylla, this new Sendera gang, whoever.

"Weapons smugglers." Manu shrugs. "Seedy, but I never met one seemed honest. It's just the business."

"Would you use them again?"

"Nah," Manu says. "Bigger chip on their shoulder than I normally like. Seem the type that business could get personal too quick. And that ain't my style."

Jaantzen nods thoughtfully. "Thank you for your input, Mr. Juric."

"Course." And because he will never learn to stop nosing around, he adds, "Friends of yours?"

Jaantzen gives him an evaluating look, and Manu assumes he won't get an answer. But, "No," Jaantzen finally says. "They came recommended by the financier."

The financier. Fascinating. Well, at least Gia wouldn't have to be pissed at Jaantzen for picking those assholes to deal with. Not that he should care, he reminds himself.

Oriol's voice comes soft from the monitors. "Oh, you're from Arquelle?"

"Shit, she's from Arquelle," Manu says. He leans closer to the screen to watch Oriol get destroyed, and to break eye contact with Jaantzen. The man's giving him a searching look — not like he knows what Manu's got planned, but something different. Something Manu can't put his finger on. It's making him uncomfortable.

"My sister just moved to Arquelle," Oriol says.

"Nonono," Toshiyo says. "More to your right."

Oriol's POV feed shifts as he leans in; on the screen, the purple-haired woman rolls her eyes, goes back to reading on her comm.

"You on-planet for long?" Oriol asks.

"Please leave me alone," the woman answers without looking up. "Or I'll call security."

"A little back to your left," says Toshiyo, leaning in to the feed with a frown. "No, left. Left left. There."

"Supposed to be a dust storm coming tonight," Oriol says, and Manu groans.

The shaky feed stabilizes at the entrance.

"All right. Get out of there, Oriol," Toshiyo says.

"Well, it was good talking to you. Enjoy your stay." Oriol's feed turns away from the woman just as she gives him another glare.

"Beni, he's on his way out," Toshiyo says.

Jaantzen steps back. "That was well done, thank you, Ms. Ravi," he says. "I'll be back shortly to go over the rest of the plan."

The knife is itching in the waistband of Manu's pants.

"Can I get a word with you, boss?" he asks. As far as pickup lines go, it's an oldie but a goodie.

Jaantzen turns to him, slow and measured like he sees all the way through the little charade Manu is trying to play.

But he nods. Buttons his suit jacket. Holds an arm out to the balcony.

The same door Kai wasn't worried he'd escape out of, the one with no exits.

Showtime.

8

TEAM PLAYER

Last time Manu was alone with Jaantzen, he wasn't standing on his own two feet like a man. He wasn't armed. He was at Jaantzen's entire mercy.

Maybe he still is, but at least he feels like he's got a better control of his destiny right now.

They walk out onto the balcony. Manu hasn't had a chance to evaluate it by daylight, but it looks like his initial examination from last night still stands: There's no way off this balcony without a fifty-foot drop to the pavement below. Kai and Gia are back in the warehouse, and neither of them will hesitate to take him out if they think he killed Jaantzen.

The only way he makes it back through that warehouse and out the door into freedom is by doing Jaantzen's job, or through some pretty fancy lying.

Fortunately, Manu's a pretty good liar.

"Mr. Juric." There's no follow-up, and Manu assumes that's Jaantzen's way of asking him what the hell he wants.

"Just wanted to ask about pay," Manu says. It's the first thing that comes to mind. "We never did go over a number."

"You'll get a cut, same as the rest of the crew."

Manu's making calculations. He's seen how fast Jaantzen is. Manu thinks he might be faster, but Jaantzen has a gun — and Manu's not sure he'll be so fast Jaantzen couldn't squeeze off a bullet. And even if Manu doesn't get hit, the second a bullet gets fired, Kai and Gia will be at the door to see what's going on.

If he wants to make his move, he needs a stronger element of surprise.

"Like a percentage, or what's the deal?"

"Flat sum," Jaantzen says. "One hundred thousand marks."

Manu lets out a low whistle, impressed in spite of himself. His suspicion from studying Jaantzen's operation has been that Jaantzen's rates are mediocre at best. The sum must be coming from the mystery financier.

"Will that be sufficient, Mr. Juric?" Jaantzen asks. "I understand it's not the half million marks you were expecting to collect, but if this job goes well there's the possibility of ongoing work."

"Sure thing," Manu says. All these numbers are meaningless to him anyway — it's not like he'll see a dime if his plan goes through. And it wasn't about the money in the first place. It was about getting into a crew. Even one as shifty as Sylla's. Had to be better than the increasing risk of getting washed out as an independent.

But the phrase "ongoing work" snags his fancy a moment, and he lets himself consider a future alongside Kai and whatever other Kai-like nasties Jaantzen has in his pocket. Manu's feeling desperate, but is he desperate enough for that?

Jaantzen still hasn't given him an opening. Manu looks out over the balcony, tries a casual position he hopes Jaantzen might imitate. The other man is still watching him like a hawk. It's like Jaantzen doesn't trust him. Big surprise.

"You aren't still considering other offers, I trust, Mr. Juric."

"Course not. But money talks."

"Are you saying that money can't buy loyalty?" Jaantzen raises an eyebrow, and in a brief moment of shock Manu realizes the big man's making a joke. "My faith in humanity is shattered," Jaantzen says, and then the eyebrow falls, the attempt at humor darkening. "I'll beat any offer your former employer made you, I promise you that. And I also promise you that if you incite a bidding war, I will kill you and anyone you love."

A chill down Manu's spine. He doesn't have many left, and if Marisa was smart she burned all ties to him once she found out what he really did. "Got it." He flashes a smile that Jaantzen does not return.

"Who put you up to the hit on me?"

"I told you I was working on my own."

"What if I told you Sylla Mar is staking out your apartment?"

Then Manu would say she has no sense of self-preservation, spreading their connection around like that. The woman has no brains. "I'd tell you she's pissed cause she asked me out and I told her no."

The corner of Jaantzen's lip quirks upwards; it takes Manu a moment to realize he's smiling. The expression is alien on Jaantzen's face, and there's something else behind it, something Manu doesn't know how to read. He's being evaluated, he can feel that. But no longer for his threat level.

"I appreciate loyalty," Jaantzen says.

Manu doesn't have a quip for that.

Talking with Willem Jaantzen all up close and personal is disconcerting. Manu's perception of the man's been turned on its head — there's that reputation for viciousness and unfairness, which Kai embodies so well. But the way his people react to him — Manu realizes he's starting to think of Toshiyo and Gia as Jaantzen's people, even if the rest are mercenary — is not what Manu expected.

Toshiyo is a mystery of a human being, and her devotion to Jaantzen seems wildly out of character given the man's reputation. Gia seems the sort of hired tough not to care, but somehow she's fiercely protective of Jaantzen.

It's all giving him pause.

Maybe the live-in lady is mellowing the grizzled gangster after all; Manu brushes the thought away. Now isn't the time to think about Jaantzen's girlfriend. Or about Toshiyo, or about Gia.

Manu is missing his chance.

Jaantzen is stepping back, out of Manu's range.

"Hey, can I give you some advice, man?" Manu calls, and it's probably a bad plan, but Jaantzen turns slowly. "Tosh is good, but she's not like the rest of us. You're gonna have to be careful with her, you think she's worth keeping around."

"I'll take your point, Mr. Juric."

He starts to walk away, and Manu knows he should shut up, but it's never been a strong point — and in the middle of a job isn't the time to pick up new habits. Plus, he's about to lose his chance. "She likes you and respects you," he says, and in Jaantzen's profile he sees a flicker of a confusion. "She'll be a good crew member."

Of all the people he's met, Willem Jaantzen is one of the hardest to read. The man's face is carved like rock but for a muscle twitching at his jawline. A wash of adrenaline floods Manu's chest and gut; the handle of the knife is digging into his kidney, and if Jaantzen turns in anger, maybe, his judgement blown by Manu's overstepping his bounds, Manu might just have the opening he needs.

But Jaantzen just turns back to study him. "Thank you," he says finally. "And would you?"

"Would I what?" Manu frowns, the moment he was supposed to have struck now lost.

"Make a good crew member."

"For the right crew, maybe."

A flurry of activity through the door, and Jaantzen turns to see who's just entered. Beni and Oriol, probably — they wouldn't have been very far out.

Jaantzen's back is broad and open, the perfect target. Manu palms the knife, steels himself to pounce. He's a heartbeat away when Jaantzen shifts and Manu can see the tall woman who's just entered the warehouse.

It's Thala Coeur.

Blackheart herself.

Manu's crisp, action-oriented adrenaline buzz drains into the high, shaky whine of catastrophe averted.

He slips his sweaty palm off the handle of the knife just as Jaantzen turns back to him. "Well, Mr. Juric. Shall we go meet the financier of this little expedition?"

Blackheart is financing this job.

"Sure thing, boss." Manu hears himself say the words, feels his face form an automatic smile. But he almost killed Blackheart's showrunner right before whatever big job she had planned.

He has a long list of people it'd suck to piss off — and a very short list of people it would be fatal to piss off.

That list is Blackheart.

Manu watches Jaantzen's broad, knife-proof back walk away.

He's not going to get another chance — and not just because of Blackheart. Manu knows, without putting a finger on exactly when it happened, that he's lost the ability to do Sylla's job.

Manu takes a deep, shaky breath and goes in to meet his newest new boss.

9

BLACKHEART

Coeur's rust-red face is impassive as she surveys the warehouse. Half her jet-black braids are woven into a crown; the tips of the rest are capped with gold and jingle as she turns her head. She's wearing slim red trousers and a black blouse that looks like real silk, light catching in soft halos where the fabric pools at her elbows and waist. She's wearing a pair of those silent bioleather training slippers, the kind worn by dancers, or boxers. Or professional thieves.

It's a deceptively soft look. Manu's never seen the woman up close, but she's famous for joining her crew in the boxing ring where they train — and for coming out on top more often than not.

The pale skin on the woman on Coeur's left is the perfect canvas for a tapestry of ink and technology that blend in an unsettling tableau. Gold-coated wires twine from ports in the right side of her shaved scalp, snaking through channels in her metal collar to their terminus in a panel set between her shoulder blades.

She's the greenest thing on New Sarjun: tattoos of jungle vines and serpents cover every exposed inch of skin on her right side, long-limbed spiders peeking from behind leaves, a wild-fanged monkey leaping from her shoulder. Her mechanical right eye seems to peer from between lush foliage.

Oh. And they're not alone, Manu realizes with a sinking heart. One last depressingly familiar face has followed Coeur in.

Jaxie. Sylla Mar's third in command.

Jaxie catches his eye, grinning.

Manu swears under his breath, but he knows true danger when he sees it. And Thala Coeur is the most dangerous thing in this room. Jaxie and Sylla will just have to wait their turn.

Before anyone can say anything, the door opens again, and it's Beni and Oriol this time, voices raised in the heat of an argument.

The jungle woman at Thala Coeur's side puts her hand on her pistol.

"It's fine," Coeur says, her voice a laughing sing-song.

Oriol lets out a string of curses.

Manu's watching the others to see if they were expecting Blackheart. Oriol's barely muffled profanity marks him as a no. Beni's jaw's on the floor — turns out he recognizes someone in the Bulari underground after all. Kai wears his sourest Kai face. Gia's scowl gets scowlier, but not in surprise. She and Coeur share a measured look, then Coeur looks past, dismissive. Manu's drama radar pings. Damn, he loves a good feud.

Toshiyo doesn't seem to register Blackheart, but she's biting her lip like she's barely holding herself back from asking the tattooed girl if she can play with her tech.

Manu tears his gaze away from Toshiyo, pushing down the sudden, nagging guilt he feels for how he used her to take down Jaantzen's guard.

Coeur's gaze skims past Manu — skims past everyone else in the room, even Jaantzen, like nobody here's worth caring who they are. He's heard that about her. You gotta prove to her it's worth bothering to learn your name.

Being beneath Blackheart's attention isn't the worst thing that could happen, though — getting her attention for the wrong reason is far, far deadlier.

Getting her attention for the right reason could be gold, though.

"I wasn't expecting a skeleton crew, Willem," she says, finally meeting Jaantzen's gaze. "Or do you have others hiding in the closet?"

"This is the crew. They'll get your job done."

Your job, huh? With Coeur in the equation, the sum Jaantzen's willing to pay makes more sense. Coeur's an extravagant spender, and her money's always good.

She shrugs, and the gold caps on the ends of her braids tinkle softly. "Then it's a good thing I brought reinforcements," she says with a half smile, like she thinks the thunderclouds gathering over Jaantzen's head are funny. She jerks a thumb at each of the new crew in turn. "Jaxie. Sarah."

Manu hears Beni's soft snort. The girl with the tech does not look like a Sarah.

Jaantzen gives Coeur a measured look. "It would have

been nice for them to be here for the initial planning," he says mildly.

Coeur just smiles, easy and bright. "Why don't you show me what you've got."

"Everybody gather around," Jaantzen says.

Manu finds a spot around the big, cheap desk in between Oriol and Beni, away from Toshiyo, and across the table from Jaxie and the other woman so he can watch them less obtrusively. Jaxie slouches into place like a regular thug, but the woman with all the tech has some element of military training to her. Could be the stiff way she holds herself, like maybe her spine is fused with robotics, too. The tattoos, Manu sees now, are there to hide a mass of scars.

She scans the table, her mechanical right eye whirring slightly as it moves. It skims past Manu, pauses on Oriol, who gives her a slight nod of respect, if not recognition. One soldier saluting another, Manu thinks, and files it away for later.

Coeur and Jaantzen stand on opposite sides of the desk, and Manu can feel the dominance game crackling through the air between them. Coeur may have hired Jaantzen to crew this job, but Jaantzen won't be acting like a hired thug.

Manu makes a mental promise not to step in between these two.

Kai, Manu notices, is mirroring Coeur's pose, though he's locked so stiff he's practically vibrating, like a mystix player trying too hard to keep from giving away a good hand. At least someone here is happy to see Blackheart.

"Good to have you all," Jaantzen says. "Ms. Ravi?"

A few clicks on the cheap desk, and Toshiyo brings up a

schematic of the neighborhood, complete with the new video feeds Oriol got them.

"We've got a better idea of what's going on in the hotel," Toshiyo says in her charming country drawl. "With our own cameras set up, we'll be first to know when the target is moving. Should be first thing tomorrow morning."

She zooms in on the hologram map; it freezes in a blur of pixels for a moment, then refreshes. "Normal couriers pick up from the side door," she says. "Word is, what we're after is getting hand-delivered out the front." She sticks a finger in the hologram. "Here."

"And where's it headed?" asks Beni.

"Along a set route," Jaantzen says, and Beni scowls at the nonanswer. Toshiyo types in a code and the route blazes green through the miniature cityscape, vanishing off the edge of the desk without revealing its terminus. Manu's not the only one frowning at the incomplete route line. Who the hell are they stealing from?

"Beni, you'll be positioned here to intercept," Jaantzen says. He sets a location pin in the hologram map, then glances up at Coeur's two new recruits. "With Manu and Jaxie. Kai will follow the courier with Oriol and Sarah. Basic smash and grab — Beni, you run him off the road. Kai pens him in from behind. Disable the driver, take the goods. Rendezvous back here."

"How do we know what to take?" asks Jaxie.

"There's only one crate," says Toshiyo. The hologram sizzles and pops. Toshiyo hits refresh. "Sandstorm's coming, sorry," she says as a loading bar appears above the map of the city. She cracks her ring fingers in unison; they sound like gunshots. Manu glances at the high windows, but of course he can see nothing.

"That's it," says Coeur. Or is she asking?

She's got an airy way with her words, like every sentence is simultaneously a jab and a challenge, her lips constantly on the edge of smiling. Like she sees what's funny and the rest of you haven't got a clue.

"That's it," says Jaantzen.

Manu expects another dominance game between them, but Coeur just steps back from the cheap desk and rolls her shoulders, nice and relaxed.

"Go get 'em, team," she says.

"Everybody rest up," Jaantzen says. "The target's moving early tomorrow, and I want you fresh."

The little crew — Manu can't decide if they're more or less motley with the addition of Sarah and Jaxie — dissolves into the vastness of the warehouse. Kai and Sarah stalk off to confer in the corner, Oriol peels off his shirt again and stakes out a section of floor for his martial arts routine, and Jaxie is watching Manu with a bald-faced "gotcha" grin. Manu turns his back on her — he's not ready to deal with that now.

"You up for a game, man?" Beni's got his deck of holocards out, shuffling them in midair with a snap. The colors shift in a rainbow blur as he bridges the deck. "C'mon. Keeps your mind sharp. And your hands."

"Not tonight," Manu says, and Beni's face falls. "Next time, yeah?" he says apologetically, even though he'd rather spend another night in Jaantzen's murder dungeon than sit through a card game. Just the thought triggers memories of his grandmother's cigars, the claustrophobia of her house, Siggy's gray face, the pointless hours wasted with incomplete decks.

"Your loss," Beni says with a shrug. He cuts the deck with one hand, and heads off to corner Gia.

Toshiyo's the only one still standing by the desk, staring at the frozen loading bar with her hands braced on the edge. Her knuckles are white.

"Hey, Tosh." Manu hovers between staying and leaving when she doesn't answer. This situation is already tangled enough without getting emotional, and the last thing he needs tonight is to indulge in his guilt. But something about the curve of her neck won't let him walk away.

He sighs, and raps his acid-green fingernails against the desk's surface. "Tosh. You doing all right, kid?"

She finally breaks eye contact with the loading bar, blinks up at him. "I'm fine," she lies.

"This isn't your type of crowd."

"Worse types out in the mines." Her accent's stronger when she says it, memory triggering the stamp of the place on her body. She crosses her arms; Manu hears the faint crack of a knuckle out of sight.

Manu frowns at that. "These are some pretty bad types."

"Not all of you. Oriol seems nice." She's got a hint of a smile in her eyes — he almost misses that she's teasing him. He wouldn't have expected it of her, not with her mind seemingly always in her devices.

He likes her, but any friendly feelings she has towards him are just going to lead to trouble for her down the road. He wants to tell her to run, to get out of this mess before it gets her killed, or locked up. Or — worse — breaks and misshapes her into any one of them.

"What are you doing here?" is what he asks instead.

"My job." It's firm. Decisive.

"You don't belong with us," Manu says. "Oriol seems nice, but he's a mercenary. Just like Gia. Just like me." He jerks his chin over his shoulder to where Sarah is locked in a menacing match of scowls with Kai. Even Beni's avoiding them for now. "Just like them."

"You're not all bad. Jaantzen — "

"We're all bad," Manu cuts in. He doesn't want to hear what she thinks about Jaantzen; it tightens the knot in his gut to know what it would have done to her if he'd finished the job an hour ago.

"I feel safe around you," Toshiyo says. "You wouldn't hurt me."

That stabs straight to the core.

"Remember what I told you about not trusting anyone here?" Manu asks, and if the words come out harsher than he intended it's because he's mad at himself more than anything. "That goes double for me, kid."

Her cheeks flame red — whether with anger, with shock, or with sadness he doesn't wait around to find out.

He feels the burn of her gaze between his shoulder blades as he walks away. Directly above the spot where the hilt of the stolen knife still digs into his back.

10

PROFESSIONALS

Manu decides to talk to Oriol. For a break — not business, just conversation. After all, he's the only one who doesn't seem to have three agendas at once. Plus, he's easy on the eyes.

He doesn't get ten steps away from Toshiyo before Jaxie catches him on an intercept course. "Fancy meeting you here," she says.

He keeps walking — Destination: Out of Earshot — and she follows along beside him. "I found you," she says, grinning like she's won first place in an amateur detective contest. Her mass of thin brown dreadlocks is tied in a messy knot at the base of her pale neck; her eyeteeth are lacquered in turquoise and trimmed with gold, filed to have just a bit more point than usual. She's dressed in casual black fatigues and prickly with her usual collection of weapons handles. Manu wonders if he can get one or two away from her.

"Surprise for sure," Manu says.

Jaxie has the presence of mind to make sure no one's listening, though her stage glance around the room screams conspiracy. Fortunately, no one's watching, either. "Word's got around the boxing gyms that Coeur and Jaantzen were looking for some people for a job. Sylla figured this was where you ended up, and when I saw you with her" — a jerk of the chin at Gia across the room — "I figured that's what happened." Jaxie grinned. "So here I am to make sure you finish your job."

Manu gives her a look. "How do you know who Gia is?" He'll stick with polite questions, but really he's dying to ask how she got to be so stupid. She'd kill Jaantzen now, with Coeur in the picture? Risk bringing that wrath down on Sylla? Blackheart'd burn Sylla's entire operation to the ground and be back home by dinner to enjoy a nice glass of wine.

"Nice reward on her head from the Alliance," Jaxie says, and Manu keeps himself from glancing over his shoulder at Gia right now. "Only reason nobody's collected it is she's thick with Jaantzen and he's tough to get through. And ain't many people want to work with the Alliance." She shrugs. "And she's a tough bitch. Hard to take her in a fight."

"That's three reasons."

Jaxie frowns at Manu like she's not sure if he's giving her shit or not.

He is.

Manu only really knows Jaxie by face and reputation — she is a predator, but slow. Sylla doesn't have much in her organization by way of brains, and Jaxie certainly doesn't add to the balance. She's not just in Sylla's crew for looks, though:

Manu's seen her fight in a friendly sparring match — "friendly" in quotations. Her opponent had to be carried away.

"Coeur know you normally work for Sylla Mar?"

"Course not," Jaxie says, but Manu doesn't believe it. Coeur didn't get to the top by being unobservant. And speaking of, she's probably observing right now. Noticing that Manu seems awfully friendly with Sylla's lackey.

Last thing he needs is for Coeur to think he's working with Sylla, because he's not — not anymore. Coeur's fortuitous arrival at the warehouse didn't just spare Jaantzen's life, it gave Manu a second chance.

Because forget Sylla Mar and her excuse for a crew.

If Manu does this job right, he could have a shot at joining the best crew in Bulari. Coeur may be scary as hell, but her crew's known as the tightest family, folks who've actually got your back so long as you do your work well. Unlike Sylla's band of opportunists.

If he can just ignore that knot in his gut.

"I'm here to make sure you finish the job," Jaxie says again, like she can sense he's slipping and the repetition will help reel him back in.

"I'll do it. After this gig is finished."

She frowns at him. "Sylla — "

"Sylla gonna pay you what this job's gonna pay?" That twitch in her cheek says no. "Then we do this job, and I make good with Sylla. All right?"

He doesn't care if she believes him or not. He leaves her standing in the middle of the room, head cocked and frowning.

Oriol is gliding effortlessly over his stretch of the warehouse floor, long, lean muscles giving an impressive display as he moves through his poses. Manu crosses his arms and leans against the wall, appreciating.

Oriol kicks out in a slow, graceful arc, spinning on the ball of one foot, his chiseled abs supporting the stance. "Did you want something?" he asks. He lunges and holds, wrists snapping into place like a dancer. His skin glistens.

"You ever get tired of flying solo?" Manu asks.

Oriol raises an eyebrow and flows into his next form. "What's there to be tired of? The independence? The not having to do shit you don't want to do?"

"The hustling for gigs. The watching your back all the time."

"I been watching my back since before you were born, boy."

Bullshit. Oriol can't have more than a decade on Manu. "How old do you think I am?" he asks.

Oriol holds his new pose just long enough to give Manu a slow smile and an appreciative look. "Old enough."

"It's the eyeliner, isn't it." Manu sighs dramatically. Oriol laughs. "Mama said it made me look older."

There's a tiny pause, and Manu almost wants him to ask: Your mama still alive? Your mama know what you do for a living? Your mama a good cook? Anything so Manu can bare a sliver of soul, say, I never knew the old lady.

But Oriol doesn't ask.

Professionals don't ask.

"You thinking of joining a crew?" is what Oriol does ask.

Manu shrugs. "Kinda have to these days. What do you know about Coeur?"

Oriol gives him a level look; Manu can't tell if he knows the dramatic adventure tale of how he was press-ganged into this little heist. "Know she prefers her people to call her Black-heart," Oriol says. "Working for her would be bread and butter." He drops into a plank, holds it effortlessly with sculpted shoulders and sinewy forearms.

Working for Coeur would be more than bread and butter — it would be a meal ticket for the rest of Manu's career. Granted, there wouldn't be anyplace to go up to, working for her. His career likely wouldn't be too long.

But it's not going to last even another month if he doesn't find himself some sort of crew. Not with the dust storm he's been stirring.

"What are you thinking?" Oriol asks, flowing into another sweeping kick. Manu catches a whiff when he moves: burnt cinnamon and gun solvent.

"That it's not fair. You ain't even breathing hard."

Oriol laughs. A leap, a handclasp, a bow, and he's finished his cycle. He grabs a towel off the edge of his cot and begins a lovely show drying off. The scar over his hipbone stands out like a rope. "I've trained since I was a kid."

"Well, your form's not too bad. There's hope for you yet." Manu pushes himself off his casual stance against the wall. "Military? That why you're so good?"

For a second he doesn't think Oriol is going to answer him — professionals don't talk — but, "Indiran Alliance," Oriol says after a moment. His attention's caught by something past Manu's shoulder, and Manu glances behind him to see the techno-thug, Sarah, talking with Kai and Gia at the other end of the warehouse.

"You and Sarah both, huh?"

Oriol frowns, as though he's not sure how Manu knew. Most people aren't aware of a fraction of the information their body language broadcasts, Manu's found.

"Yeah, looks like," Oriol says. "Tech like what she's got isn't normally civilian." He tosses aside the towel and pulls on a shirt, then sits on his cot. Manu sits across from him, not waiting for invitation.

"You serve out your indenture?"

"Disability discharge. Then an old buddy needed some security and I needed some cash. And now?" Oriol doesn't say more, just waves a hand around the warehouse as if to say, *And this is where I ended up.*

Manu doesn't have to ask about the injury. The way Oriol's thumb started rubbing his hip, it must be whatever intriguing scar runs below his waistband. Maybe after all this wraps up Manu will get a chance to learn more about it. He sincerely hopes so.

"How about you?"

"Me? Nah, no military for me."

Oriol rolls his eyes. "I can see that, kid. I meant how did you get into the business?"

Marisa's the only person Manu's ever told the truth to. They'd finally had the "This is what I do, this is how I got here" conversation, which ended with her begging him to get out of the business, him refusing, and her parents calling the cops. Good times.

"My cousin got in with this abusive asshole a few years back," he says before he regrets not saying it. "She got pregnant and tried to leave him, so he killed her." Manu clears his throat. "He was my first hit."

Oriol whistles, low. "Good for you."

Manu hasn't told this story enough to dull it up yet, and he didn't expect the stab of pain, like the moment's still fresh-cut and razor-sharp. Those guilty feelings about Toshiyo must be dredging up company; Manu's having trouble pushing back the memory of Siggy's papery palm cooling in his hand.

For one wild moment he wants desperately to turn Oriol into a confessor. To peel back a little of the bandage and show the wound — like he tried to do with Marisa before that all blew up in his face. I tried to tell her he was no good, he wants to say, or, I figured if she could handle her dad all those years she could handle him, or, She told me she loved him.

But Oriol? Oriol's a professional.

Manu's a professional.

"Too little too late," is what Manu finally says, with a wave of his hand. "Anyway, turns out the asshole was in deep with a local gang and they had a bounty out on him. They paid me off and asked if I'd work another job for them. Not like I had anything else going on, so I said yes." He spreads his arms. "Almost five years later, look at me. Working with the best."

"I'm flattered."

Manu winks. "I was talking about Blackheart."

Oriol doesn't return his levity. "I know you were," he says, and for a moment there's something weary behind his gaze. "Tell you what, kid. You wanna join a crew, that's your call. Just don't do anything stupid to get on some boss's good side."

Way too late for that.

Manu wants to ask why, pry at that tiny chink in Oriol's armor. For a moment, the way Oriol's watching him, Manu thinks he might even just answer.

But that kind of intimacy isn't just frowned upon by professionals — it's dangerous. Distracting.

"Thanks for the advice, old-timer," is what Manu says, and the moment is gone.

Oriol shakes his head in faux outrage. "Old-timer? How old do you think I am?"

"Not too old." Manu glances over his shoulder. "But old enough to see we're not being told everything about what's going on."

A shrug. "Of course we aren't. Name of the game. Here." Oriol reaches into the duffel at the foot of his bed, pulls out a clear bottle filled with brown liquid. It's a familiar label — not the cheapest whiskey, but not the priciest, either. Something Manu himself would have bought.

He takes the offered bottle and Oriol's fingers brush up against his companionably. Oriol's watching him, those honey-gold eyes catching the light.

Manu smiles. Sips. Hands it back. "What's next for you?" he asks.

"I never think about the next job in the middle of the current job," he says.

"That's not true," Manu says. "Everybody's always got the next plan brewing. You got somebody waiting back for you, or what's next?"

"Thought I might lie low for a while. Get some relaxation on somewhere."

"That sounds good."

"I know it does. You oughta think about the same."

"Is that an invitation?"

Oriol just shrugs, but the way he tilts his head says yes.

"I'll check my calendar," Manu says.

Manu almost doesn't hear it when she calls, that tentative alto not quite rising above the rest of the group's clamor. He lifts a hand, and Oriol falls silent beside him.

"Uh, guys?" Toshiyo calls again, a little louder this time. She hasn't left the cheap desk, and she's hunched over her strange hand terminal, eyes wide with worry. Manu's halfway across the room before he realizes he's moving; across the warehouse, Jaantzen shoulders past Kai.

"What is it?" Jaantzen's voice booms where hers is timid, and the rest of the chatter in the warehouse fades away.

"They're on the move," Toshiyo says. "It's showtime."

11

WE'RE A GO FOR TROUBLE

"Now?" That's Kai.

Toshiyo just blinks at him. She's thumbing commands into her hand terminal with her right hand, cupping her left over her ear to help her listen in better to whatever she's got going on.

"Now?" Kai growls again.

"Let her work," Manu snaps, and Kai rounds on him with teeth bared.

"Let her work," a voice echoes, and Manu's surprised to see it's Coeur. She glances at him only briefly as she turns to study Toshiyo. Kai falls silent beside her, chin dropping.

Well.

Manu glances at Jaantzen, but he doesn't seem to notice his bulldog's come to heel for Coeur.

"The courier company's moving the package," Toshiyo

says, ignoring everyone except for the voices in her earpiece and whatever she sees on her hand terminal.

"Have they changed routes?" Jaantzen asks.

"No, boss. Just delivery times."

"Why?"

"Not sure. Could be because of the storm coming in."

"You find out, you let me know."

"Yeah, boss."

"Then the job's still on as discussed," Jaantzen says. "Kai, Oriol, you're with Sarah in the truck. Manu, Jaxie, you're with Beni."

Manu catches the earpiece Gia tosses him — they're all getting one, except for Sarah, who taps a sequence into her gauntlet. Oriol's popped a caffeine tab under his tongue; he sees Manu notice and offers up the package. Manu shakes his head. Caffeine doesn't play well with his natural adrenaline, and he's got plenty of that going at the moment.

"Where's she going?" Jaxie says, thumbing over her shoulder at Gia.

"Gia's either making sure you don't get shot up, or fixing you if you do," says Jaantzen. "Your choice."

"I'll take the former," Manu says.

"Then you best stop testing me, boy," Gia answers. She tosses the last of the earpieces to Jaxie and grins at Manu; she looks like the goddess of war on the eve of battle. How this one was ever accepted to a religious academy like Sulila is beyond him. "Here," she says, and hands him a thumb-sized neural stunner. "I been saving this for you."

Manu turns it over in his palm: it's a matte-black rubber bracelet with a pair of nodes on the side about fifteen millimeters apart. It's the type off-planet women wear discreetly on their wrists when they go out slumming in Bulari. Manu lifts an eyebrow at Gia. "Gee. Thanks."

"Less mess when you deal with the driver," she says. She's got one on her own wrist, like she couldn't just knock any asshole out with one good punch from her well-muscled arms.

No one asks where Coeur is going to be — far away and out of the line of fire is what's understood. Manu's surprised she even bothered to show up at the warehouse, and wonders again just what's in this shipment.

None of his business, is what.

Manu pops in his earpiece and has a strange out-of-body sensation as Toshiyo speaks both in his ear and across the desk.

"Testing," says Toshiyo, repeating herself as they gear up. She frowns at Sarah. "Do you — "

"I gotcha," Sarah says, tapping a finger on the panel behind her right ear. "Loud and clear." Toshiyo stares at her in naked fascination.

"All right. I'll be keeping an eye on the transport from here and direct you where to go."

They break apart into teams; as Manu's waiting for Jaxie and Beni to finish suiting up, he spots Coeur standing by herself, the light pooling in the soft drape of her black silk blouse to highlight the topography of muscles beneath. Her arms are crossed; the long, scarred red-brown fingers of one hand tap an impatient rhythm.

Manu licks his lips, makes the move. "Wanted to say thank you for the opportunity," he says, and Coeur's gaze drifts onto him like a feather, light and impermanent; he's no threat to her.

She's drinking him in, filing him away, and Manu stays relaxed, lets his body fall into the same casual stance as hers, mirroring the angle of her hips, his hands in his pockets. Not a troublemaker — he's useful. Friendly.

"Good to see new talent," she says finally. "You and me, we'll talk when this is all over. I like me some fresh blood from time to time."

"Sounds good," he says, with little bow of his head to show he appreciates she's doing him a favor.

His pride should be buzzing — he's getting the green light from his dream boss — but it's not untying that knot in his gut.

He glances back at the desk and sees Toshiyo watching him, disappointment clear on her face. When he meets her gaze, she looks away and does not turn back.

Manu shakes it off. It's not like he was on her side, or Jaantzen's side, or even Sylla's side. Maybe Coeur's side's a bit rotten, but it's no worse than any other.

And if so, then why does he feel no better than his grandma? Choosing poorly by failing to choose at all?

Goddamn this job and what it's dredged up.

"Manu."

He spins to find Gia, grateful for the interruption of his thoughts.

"I grabbed this from your gear," she says, and slips a package into his hand. He pockets it without looking, knowing by touch that familiar roll of adhesive-backed tags and minia-ture remote controller. The last of his hornet tags. Manu grins.

"I already regret giving you this," Gia says. "You look way too happy."

"I'll do you proud," he says, and gets only a shaking head in return.

"Just keep yourself off my table."

"Got it, Giaconda."

He winks and walks away before she can answer. Jaxie and Beni are waiting for him, now; Beni shouts at him from the door to hurry up.

"Good luck," Coeur calls to Jaantzen, and her brilliant smile beams a fraction of a second too slow. No love lost there, Manu realizes. But then, what he hears, there's no love lost between anyone in the business and Jaantzen.

Except for Toshiyo.

And except for Gia; Manu sees her solemn nod to the big gang boss as she walks past.

Manu gives him a deep nod, too. Respectful. He means it, no matter what brought them together and where their paths may go from here.

"Good luck," Manu says to Toshiyo, and gets only a cool look in return.

He tells himself it's a good thing. That he's only helping sour her on a business she shouldn't be in in the first place.

He tells himself that no matter what he's heard about Jaantzen, the man seems to honestly care about Toshiyo. And anyway, Gia's got her back — and she's the fiercest woman he's ever met.

He feels like shit.

12

HEISTING

It's dark outside, dusty, a sandstorm blowing down from the desert and into the Bulari Valley so that the whole city is blanketed in a faint haze. It probably made for a romantic blood-red sunset from the decks of high-rise tourist bars earlier this evening, but now it's got plans for mischief. Manu can't tell if the constant rumble of cargo shuttles and magtrucks out of the spaceport is shut down, what with the wind. Probably.

Manu coughs; beside him, Jaxie sneezes in a series of short, ridiculous bursts. When she gets herself under control she gives the rest of the group a feral glare, light glinting off her turquoise-and-gold incisors. No one comments.

Manu's got a nice breathing mask back at his apartment, one of the better biosilk ones, but he hadn't brought it with him to bust up the Bronze Room. He hadn't realized he was going to get into such a fun new adventure.

He'll be better prepared next time.

He gives Oriol a salute, then lets Jaxie shoulder past him to take the front seat in Beni's spinner. He'd rather be in the back keeping an eye on them, anyway.

Out into the road, and Beni's driving fast and loose while Toshiyo's voice echoes through their earpieces with updates on the courier's route. Beni handles the spinner like the pro Jaantzen said he was — Manu guesses all those games of cards must indeed be good for the mind and the hands.

Jaxie lets out another round of the ridiculous sneezes, bitches about hating sandstorms. Manu ignores her.

Their position is marked by a glowing green dot in the faint hologram of the city superimposed over the windshield, but once Manu gets his bearings he doesn't need to follow it to know where they are.

This is his city and he's in the zone, following their route in his mind even as his vision glazes at the flashing images outside the window. Store lights are soft glows in the haze.

Manu's never been off-world — hell, he's never left Bulari — and he's not sure he wants to. But something about Oriol's soft accent, and the idea of emerald rice paddies and actual oceans sending in storms and hurricanes rather than the whirling dust storms sent in by the Jupari Desert — it sounds awfully nice right about now.

"He just reached Pioneer Plaza, turning left onto Mahti Drive."

Toshiyo's voice comes staticky through his earpiece, bringing him back to the moment. They're getting close — he blinks to refocus his eyes and lets the blur outside resolve into familiar scenery.

Beni takes a sharp right into an alley; Manu sways with the motion of the spinner. In the front seat, Jaxie is muttering to herself as she checks her weapons.

"Hold tight," Beni says, and Manu digs into the hand-holds. Beni skids the spinner around the corner, drifting into the path of the courier van. Manu braces himself for impact, but the van skids to a halt, swerving to miss Beni and crashing into a low retainer wall with a screech and a spark of electronics.

Beni dances the spinner out of range as a second crash sounds — Sarah's vehicle smashing into the back of the van.

Manu's first out of the spinner, guns up to cover the driver. Smoke is pouring out of the engine, out of the cab, and the man stumbles out hacking. He's got a lightweight pistol in his hand, but he's too disoriented by the smoke and the crash to do more than wave it through the air in front of him.

"Drop it," Manu yells, and the man's eyes widen as the smoke clears enough for him to register Manu's guns and Jaxie's hefty stun carbine. He sets the pistol carefully on the ground; Jaxie scoops it up, shoves it in her belt.

The area is secluded, mostly warehouses and industrial businesses, but it won't be long before someone comes to investigate the noise. Manu hopes Gia had enough time to get in position and warn them if she sees anything.

"He alone?" Manu shouts to Jaxie, who's prodding at the smoke boiling out of the cab with the glowing tip of her stun carbine. "You alone?" he asks the driver.

The driver coughs, refusing to answer.

"He left alone," Toshiyo says in his ear; he thinks she

says — the static is getting worse as the storm intensifies. "Secure him . . . back help the others."

"All clear in here," Jaxie yells, hopping down from the cab.

Manu zaps the driver with the neural stunner — it's got a bigger, more satisfying kick than he expects — then he and Jaxie each grab one of the driver's arms, hauling him away from the smoldering ruin of his courier van to prop him against a warehouse grate.

Manu reaches across his chest to cuff him, and the man's jacket falls open. Manu can see the edge of what looks like a badge: concentric circles on a blood-red background. He shoves the jacket open the rest of the way to be sure.

Alliance.

Shit.

"Shit!" Jaxie's eyes are wide. "Should I kill him?"

"How are you such an idiot?" Manu says.

He ignores the daggers she's glaring his way. Trigger-happy psycho has no sense of how consequences play out no matter what the game, apparently. He snaps the cuffs into place and frisks the man for weapons, electronics, anything. Not that it matters much what he finds — the call was probably sent automatically as soon as the van crashed. And a whole swarm of Alliance special security ops will be on them in a minute.

"We need to tell the others," Manu says. He's on Jaxie's heels as they jog to the back of the courier van. Kai and Oriol are securing a bulky crate in the back of Sarah's van.

"Driver's down," Manu shouts. "But we gotta go. He — "

He's interrupted by screeching tires and whirls, pistols out. But it's just Beni's spinner, speeding away to the rendezvous like he didn't have passengers he was supposed to take with him.

Manu swears.

"I guess we're riding with you," he says to Sarah, and she just glares at him and thumbs at the narrow, hard benches lining both walls of the van.

Dammit, Manu hates this job.

Sarah's starting to pull away before Manu even has a chance to close the back door.

"Drive!" Jaxie growls. "The driver had a fucking Alliance badge."

Well, Manu no longer needs to decide if he's going to mention that or not. He manages to get one arm through a safety harness before Sarah lurches the van into her first corner. "Did you know we were hitting the Alliance?" Manu asks Oriol and Kai. Kai just ignores him.

"I don't ask," Oriol says with a hint of impatience.

Manu clicks his microphone on. "Tosh? Did you know we — "

Something clicks out on his feed. He frowns at Kai, but it's Sarah who's tapping something into her gauntlet.

She hits a button and his earpiece comes back to life with a dry pop. He can hear Toshiyo on the other end: "Manu? Manu, what happened? Come in."

"Tosh, the courier was Alliance. Get out of there." But he can tell his words aren't getting through.

"Manu?"

"He's good," says Kai, and Manu can hear Toshiyo's sharp intake of breath. "Communication troubles. Sandstorm."

Sarah clicks off the connection again.

"What did you do?" Manu asks.

"Time for radio silence," Sarah says.

"What the fuck is going on?"

"New plan," Kai says. "Alliance got told where the base was."

"Told by who?" Manu asks.

Kai doesn't answer. "Change of rendezvous. Beni, come in." He taps at his earpiece. "Get me back with Beni," he tells Sarah. "Chump took off too fast. And hail Gia. We need her to meet us."

Jaxie makes a face at Manu, but then just straps herself into the harness without a word. She's game for anything.

Oriol says nothing, but he meets Manu's gaze with a small frown. This is all news to him, and he's not happy about the change in plans.

"Base needs to know," Manu says. But Kai and Sarah have obviously hijacked this job — whether they're going out on their own, or working with Coeur to double-cross Jaantzen. He wants to live, he needs to keep his mouth shut. "If the Alliance is on their way to the warehouse, we have to tell base."

"Not your problem," Kai says.

Oriol's shaking his head, Shut up, kid written all over his face.

"Yes, ma'am," Sarah says in answer to some call only she can hear. "We have the crate. Heading to the second rendezvous point."

Coeur it is, then. They're heading to the second rendezvous to meet with Coeur, who has set Toshiyo and Jaantzen up to take the fall with the Alliance.

And his first job as her new potential recruit is to let them.

"You can't leave them to get picked up," Manu says, even though that's clearly what Kai and Sarah intend to do.

"We got orders," Kai says, his voice barely more than a growl.

Manu doesn't care.

"What the hell is in this box Coeur wants so bad?" he asks, slipping out of his harness.

Kai lunges for him, but Manu's already pried the lid off the box. It comes loose more easily than he expected, and he lurches back, spine cracking against the bench.

"You guys knock it off back there," Sarah yells, swerving — out of necessity or emphasis, Manu can't tell which.

Manu pulls himself gingerly into a crouch, but Kai isn't coming after him — he's staring at whatever's in the box, his face a mask of fury. A flush of red seeps out from his collar and hairline, and Manu'll bet he's about to see real-life steam pouring out of the man's cauliflower ears.

"What the hell?" That's Oriol, his professional expression fractured into confusion.

Manu pushes himself up to see.

What's in the box is Beni: limp, but breathing, folded up like a rag doll, his neck cricked at an uncomfortable angle.

And on that neck, two welts, about fifteen millimeters apart — like the marks Manu's neural stunner just left on the neck of the courier driver.

"I saw Beni driving away," Jaxie says, brow furrowed in confusion.

Manu also saw Beni's spinner tearing away. He never for a minute thought Beni wasn't at the controls.

"So who was driving?" Jaxie asks.

Kai lets out a deadly growl.

"Gia."

13

BACKING UP THE BACKUP PLANS

"Which way did she go?" Sarah yells, and Manu grabs a handhold just as she swerves to the right. He tumbles onto a bench and grabs at the harness, trying three times to get the buckles to catch. Oriol's done the same across the way.

"Hail her!" Kai yells back.

"I'm trying. She's not answering."

"Of course she's not answering," Manu says, and for a split second he gets a face full of Kai's red-eyed fury. Oriol's giving him a warning look. "If she and Jaantzen were planning to double-cross the rest of us the whole time, you think she'll answer now?"

Sarah spits out a string of profanity and veers to the left.

"She'll have a backup plan with Toshiyo and Jaantzen," Manu says. He's staring down the bull; he can feel Kai's breath hitting his cheek in hot, angry blasts, but he doesn't care anymore: Cut me again, asshole, he thinks. He's over these games.

"They're the only ones who can bring Gia in, now," Manu says. "Unless they get taken by the Alliance."

Kai and Sarah share a glance.

"Unless you think I'm wrong, and Gia's actually working with Blackheart. You think Blackheart was planning to leave us all out to dry all along?"

That gets results. Manu's gratified to see righteous fury on Kai's face, and can't believe Jaantzen got taken for a sucker by this one. Everything about his body language screams traitor. He wishes now that he'd said something, but how could he have known?

Thing is, it's not a matter of whether or not he could have known — he knew the whole time. Knew by their body language that Kai was loyal to Coeur and that Coeur wouldn't think twice about throwing Jaantzen to the wolves. Knew in his gut that Marisa would leave him the second she found out what he did. Knew by reputation that Siggy's deadbeat boyfriend would kill her if she tried to leave.

He just hadn't done a damn thing about it. Just like his grandma'd never done a damn thing about what her sons did to either of her grandkids.

Oriol's trying his best to stay out of the argument. Checking his weapons, reloading a magazine. Jaxie's hanging with one arm hooked through her harness, watching Kai and Manu like she's at a boxing match but doesn't have money on the line. Nobody's paying any attention to Beni. Poor bastard's gonna have a bad day when he wakes up.

The Alliance is closing in on Toshiyo and Jaantzen, and nobody else is going to help them out.

"You wanna get Blackheart her due, you better track down Gia," Manu says. "And Jaantzen and Toshiyo are the only ones who can do that."

A long beat. Kai's glare slowly morphs into frustration as he realizes Manu is right.

"Pull over," he barks at Sarah. "Base, you copy?"

Sarah screeches to a halt in an alleyway, then taps something in her gauntlet. The maneuver makes Oriol drop a bullet. He gives Sarah a mild-mannered look that on another man might be fury, then reaches long golden fingers to pick it back up, snap it into the magazine.

"All right. You're on," Sarah says.

"Base, you copy?" Kai asks again.

Toshiyo's voice crackles through all of their ears. "Kai! What happened?"

"Target was Alliance — I think we got played. You two get out of there."

A faint hesitation. Manu shouts at Toshiyo in his mind: Listen! Get out of there!

"Copy that," Toshiyo says finally. "Rendezvous two."

"Good," Kai says. "Gia, you copy? Rendezvous two."

"I'll make sure she and Beni know. I'll still be — shit — "

Toshiyo cuts out in a staccato of gunfire.

Manu's heart sinks.

Rendezvous Two is even dingier and less impressive than the

original warehouse, and about twenty minutes away. They pull into an oversized garage, the sort of place you could strip down and refurb an entire orbital cargo hauler. Given the stink of oil and jagged piles of thruster parts stacked haphazardly around the room, that's probably exactly what it's been used for.

Manu's the first one out of the van — he's been having trouble breathing since they lost Toshiyo, but the stench of mechanics and dust in the garage isn't making things any easier. He scans the room, sneezes. Scans the room.

Sneezes.

"What the fuck is this place," he mutters. He's aware how pissy he sounds. He needs to dial it back.

Oriol steps out beside him, and Manu can feel his evaluating gaze. Oriol's deciding if he needs to distance himself. They share a brief glance, but Oriol just goes back to scanning the room. He's chosen sides from the beginning, and that side is Team Oriol. Manu shrugs it off.

"Help me get this guy out," he says to Jaxie. Beni's still crowded into the box, and nobody's thought to do a thing about it. Not even Manu, until just this second, so he doesn't give himself any hero points, either.

Beni wakes up as they pry him out, head lolling and muscles loose. "It's okay, big guy," Manu says. "You're gonna be fine."

"Zheeee."

"It's okay."

Manu and Jaxie stretch him awkwardly on the floor of the van, stand to go. Beni grabs for Jaxie's arm, misses, grabs again and claws his fingers in her sleeve. She looks like she might hit him. "Zheee," he says, his speech a blur of vowels on his stunned tongue. She tugs away and he lets out a desperate, frustrated moan.

"It was Gia," Manu tells him. "We know."

Beni slumps back, message delivered. He doesn't try to move again as Manu and Jaxie leave him lie.

"What now," Manu snaps at Kai as he climbs back out of the van. He can't keep the anger out of his voice, even though he knows he'll be no help to Toshiyo and Jaantzen if he pisses Kai off so much the man shoots him before they even get here.

If they're even still alive.

"Now we wait," Kai says. He gives Manu a long, evaluating look. "You got a problem with that?"

"No problems," Oriol answers for him. Manu swings his head to meet the other man's gaze, and those honey-gold eyes pierce sharp. "Do we?" Oriol says, quiet.

"No problems," Manu says.

None that'll do him any good to bring up now, at least. He shrugs on his jacket. "I'll check out the perimeter," he says, and walks away before anyone can stop him. Behind him, he can hear Oriol murmuring something to Kai, defusing the situation. Whatever it is, it makes Sarah laugh.

Rendezvous Two is all fourth-wave architecture, around the era when prefab warehouse panels were first being constructed on New Sarjun instead of being slung across the void from Indira. Got that signature gray-yellow patina from the early industrial metal composites corroding over time. Replicas of this look are popular in bars in the tourist district — the more dedicated to colonist kitsch the bar, the pricier the shots of imported Indiran liquors.

Nobody's setting up a swanky bar in this place, though — not without some serious bribes paid to the Bulari health department. Manu slaps his palm on the cracked glass beside the door and feels it shift. It's been covered over in a peeling, yellowing film. Probably the only thing keeping it together for now.

Someone's been living here, though they're not home now. There's a pile of trash in the corner, picked through and sorted into careful piles. A few moped frames stripped of their parts. Nothing to indicate that whoever normally lives here is into anything bigger than petty theft and dropping shard.

Manu tries a light switch. The archaic electrical system doesn't seem to be working, but Manu pats the side of a circuit box as he passes.

"Anything to report?"

He turns just as Jaxie exhales a cloud of cigarette smoke. It doesn't improve the warehouse's general eau de dusty oil fume.

Manu points at the pile of blankets in the corner. "We have a fellow trespasser."

Jaxie's pulse carbine snaps to hands, the cigarette dangling from her lips.

"Relax, psycho. He's not here."

She shoots him a dirty look and lowers the gun.

"We just supposed to meet them here?" he asks, and Jaxie shrugs. He tries to ignore the elephant in the room, that Jaantzen and Toshiyo are probably in the custody of the Alliance as they speak. Best say your goodbyes, if that's the case. Get caught stealing from the Alliance it's a trip to

Redrock, for sure — and Manu doesn't know anyone who's ever gotten out of Redrock.

Except for Gia.

He desperately hopes she's out there doing something heroic.

A glass sign over the door reads Office. Manu gives a little hop and slaps it as he walks past. Jaxie gives him a look. "For good luck," he says.

"I didn't know you were superstitious."

"Learned it from Grannie."

"Grannies don't always teach the best lessons," says a man's voice behind him. Rich baritone, and Manu spins with weapon in hand, not sure what sort of reception he'll be receiving. Across the room he hears safeties clicking off, Kai's grunt and swear. Beside his shoulder, the faint whine of Jaxie's pulse carbine.

It's Jaantzen and Toshiyo; he's carrying a briefcase in each hand, she's clutching a backpack clunky with bulky angles. His expression is dark.

"Nice to see you all, too," he says.

14

KILL SHOT

Manu lowers his weapon a fraction, sees the others do the same. Guns don't go back in holsters, though, and Manu doesn't think anyone is fooled by the faux civility.

He honestly didn't expect Jaantzen to show up here — the fact that he'd been betrayed must have been painfully obvious, and he's not an idiot. But here he is, playing right into Coeur's hands. Manu has a sick feeling about this.

Jaantzen walks slowly through the room, Toshiyo trailing behind him with wide eyes. Her grip slips on the awkward backpack and Manu has to stop himself from grabbing it from her and shouldering the load. He needs his hands free for whatever's about to happen.

He needs her out of here.

"We've got to track down Gia," he says. "She — "

"She knocked Beni out and took the goods," Kai cuts in.

His glare makes it clear he doesn't trust Manu not to let something slip.

Everything has slipped, asshole.

"Why would she do that?" Jaantzen asks in mock surprise.

"You told her to," Kai growls, and Jaantzen doesn't deny the obvious. "You double-crossing us?"

The slight hint of amusement on Jaantzen's face hardens. "I'm doing the job I was hired for, Kai. I'm not sure I can say the same for you."

The veins in Kai's thick neck are pulsing hard. Manu clears his throat before speaking — he doesn't want to get a bullet in the head.

"There's a table here where Tosh can set up her gear," Manu says, pointing to a workbench away from the van, away from the action. Away from trouble. Kai and Jaantzen both glare at him.

"She can call Gia where she is," Kai says. Toshiyo starts to set down the backpack, and Kai swings his gun back to cover her. "Slow," he says.

Manu sighs. "Seriously, man, she — "

"Shut up or I kill you," Kai says.

There's an edge in Kai's voice beyond the anger, and even Sarah's glaring at him now, her mechanical eye scanning him independent of the biological one. Manu wonders what she sees.

The edge in Kai's voice is a sort of dizzy power that Manu has heard over and over in his life from people who believed they were finally throwing off some sort of imagined oppression. It's the same sort of fever pitch his dad's voice would take on when he'd been drinking, just before the blows began to land. But Manu doesn't think Kai's been drinking. And that just makes this moment even more dangerous.

Toshiyo's bag meets cement with a heavy clatter as the equipment inside shifts against itself. She slides her fingerprint along the seal and a faint heat trail follows behind. Unlocked.

"Show me," Kai says, and she looks confused for a second, starts to reach in.

"Show him what's in the bag," Manu says. He'd like to say more, but Kai shoots him a dangerous look.

Manu's mind is racing. Everybody has triggers: say the right word and they'll smile at a shared memory, laugh at a joke, or fly into a rage. It's how he kept Marisa around for so much longer than she should have stayed, even though they were terrible for each other — knowing just how to defuse an argument, how to make her smile again. It's how he worked his dad's anger to shift his attention when all the body language screamed danger. How he knew exactly when to ask his grandma for a favor.

And how he's learned when to get the hell out of the way.

Every cell of his body is screaming that now is one of those times.

Manu doesn't know Kai well enough to know his triggers, but he can tell he thinks he's on the edge of something big. The way he's peacocking on power, chest out and chin up, the lazy way he's swinging the weapon back and forth, Manu guesses he's been waiting to get the upper hand on Jaantzen a long time.

Two days ago, Manu Juric would be standing back to see

where the bullets landed, then walking out with the winners. Today, he's choosing sides.

And the side he's choosing is the one currently having the guns pointed at their heads.

Marisa was right: He makes terrible decisions.

Toshiyo yawns the mouth of the bag towards Kai, whose expression goes all brow-overhang and pursed lips; he can't make heads nor tails of the mess inside. Neither can Manu, but it's clearly not a gun or a bomb. Kai waves her on.

Toshiyo pulls her complicated-looking hand terminal out of the bag and thumbs it on, touches her earpiece as though waiting for it to pair, which it certainly should have done already. She cracks both ring fingers.

Manu frowns.

Seriously? Is Toshiyo Ravi acting?

He starts to interject again, give Toshiyo that extra second before Kai wonders why things are taking so long, but Jaantzen speaks first.

"What is it you were unhappy with, Kai?" Jaantzen asks. "The pay? The hours?"

Kai's weapon is still trained on Toshiyo, though his attention swings to Jaantzen. Sarah frowns at him. Jaxie shifts her weight. Oriol's standing loose and ready. Though for what, Manu isn't sure.

"What?" Kai asks.

"You and I, we've worked together for years. What did Coeur offer you that I couldn't? Better pay? Benefits?"

"She didn't have to offer me anything," Kai says. "You think you're so smart, but I know you came from Brightby orphanage just the same as me. You think you're so posh in your suits and your fancy wines, but you ain't nothin more than what I am. Then you think you can buy me like I'm some indentured goon."

"I never tried to buy you," Jaantzen says. His gaze is level, even. His hands are out straight, but his right hand wants badly to slip under his coat. Manu can tell by the angle, by how much closer he holds it, by the ever-widening gap between the thumb and the forefinger while the left stays still as a statue. Kai doesn't seem to notice. "I don't do indentures."

"'I don't do indentures,'" Kai says, mocking. "You never done an indenture, you don't know what it's like to make that choice. Lookin down on the rest of us who've done it like it's dirty. It's the fuckin way of life."

Jaantzen frowns slightly at that, and it's genuine. "You would've preferred I put you under contract?"

Not the time for this conversation. Manu screams at him in his brain, because he can see Willem Jaantzen is genuinely curious about Kai's employment preferences, and Kai is only curious about how good it'll feel to finally pull the trigger.

"Making decisions like you're a god, like you're so fucking smart, when what have you done but wore fancy clothes and send others to do your dirty work?"

"Didn't I pay you well?"

"Fuck you." Kai swings his weapon up for a kill shot.

Toshiyo cries out.

Manu pulls his trigger.

15

TOO MUCH DRAMA

Kai falls, a slow topple back, a stray bullet squeezed from his gun past Jaantzen's leg, a shower of sparks as it ricochets off the bag of machinery in front of Toshiyo.

Manu waits for the bullet that will take him, from Sarah, behind them — he hears her swear — but Oriol is faster. He lets a spray of bullets fly as he dives for cover. Manu spins to take her out, but it's Jaantzen's shot that catches her straight between the eyes.

Manu aims his pistol at Jaxie's head. "You do and you're dead," he says.

She lowers her pulse carbine, raises a hand. "We good, man."

It's over as soon as it began.

Oriol stands carefully, scanning the room behind them, his weapon at the ready. "Shit, man," he says. "This is too much fucking drama."

"I'll split Kai's and Sarah's cuts between the three of you if you stay on my crew until we're through," says Jaantzen, pistol still in his hand, evaluating Oriol's trustworthiness. Evaluating all their trustworthiness.

Oriol lifts a golden eyebrow. "Cut of what? This deal gone south, man." But he's not casing Jaantzen, he's turned and is watching the room, body language tense but casual. He'll take the offer, even if he doesn't like it.

"My crew gets paid," Jaantzen says. His hand's on his pistol, his finger on the trigger. His eyes are painting a target on the back of Oriol's neck.

"He's good," Manu says. Jaantzen glances at him. Manu gives him a nod. "And Jaxie's good."

"She's one of Coeur's."

"She's with Sylla Mar," Manu says, and Jaxie lets out an angry yelp. Jaantzen doesn't look surprised, and Manu wonders if he's known all along, or if he's just not that easy to rattle. He suspects the latter. "We're in." He gets an irritated side-eye from Oriol, but no argument. "Tosh, you all right?"

There's no answer. Behind him, Jaantzen lets out a curse.

Manu spins to find Toshiyo slumped on the floor, hands pressed to her side, covered in blood. Her eyelids flutter weakly. Manu grabs an extra shirt from his gear bag and kneels beside her, carefully peels back her fingers to press it over the wound. "Stay with me, Tosh," he says. "Gia's on her way."

A quick glance up at Jaantzen to confirm — he's already on his comm.

"Blackheart knows where we are," says Oriol. He's kneeling beside Sarah's body, checking through her clothes.

"Thousand marks says she got an alert when cyborg-gal bit it. We need — ah, here." He tugs something free from her shoulder and holds it up to the light: a hard plastic vial half filled with silvery liquid.

"What is that?"

"Coag nanites. Part of the automatic tech system."

"How do you know?"

"You ain't seen me naked yet. Get me a vein, man."

"Boys." Jaantzen holds out his hand for the vial; Oriol hands it over, then opens up his small medkit and pulls out a syringe. He holds out his hand for the vial, but Jaantzen is still staring at it. "What will this do to her, Mr. Sina?"

"Fix her enough that we can move her." Jaantzen's still waiting. "I ain't working for Blackheart, I'm working for a living," says Oriol. "Your name's on my contract, and Tosh's the one who's gonna get us payday." He shrugs. "Plus, unless any of the rest of you've patched up a bullet wound in the middle of combat . . . ?"

Manu has her sleeve rolled up by the time Oriol's gotten the vial back from Jaantzen and kneels beside him. The heat off his shoulder is a stark contrast to Toshiyo's cool arm.

"Press your thumbs there, Manu. K, Tosh, I need you to squeeze your hand," says Oriol. The silver liquid swirls like smoke as Oriol finds the vein and depresses the syringe. "Good girl. Manu, hold her tight a sec. The first minute can be pretty shitty." Oriol grabs Toshiyo's legs, leaning his weight down just as she starts to kick. "Sorry, Tosh."

Manu spares a glance up at Jaantzen, but he's scanning the room, apparently deciding to trust them after all. "Get on the door," Jaantzen says to Jaxie. "Gia's on her way."

"So's Blackheart," says Oriol again. "We're gonna sit you up, kiddo." Toshiyo's tremors are starting to subside, and Oriol's got a miniature spray can of wound sealant to replace Manu's blood-soaked shirt. The foam stiffens into a pliable shield, but he winds a sterile wrap around her torso to hold it in place anyway. "Your color's better. How's your pain?"

"Fucking hurts," Toshiyo says, the words rasping tight between her teeth.

"Yeah, that happens. Only thing I got in my kit's gonna knock you out. And I don't think we can afford you knocked out just yet."

"I'll be fine," Toshiyo says. Oriol smiles back, but it's only for show, Manu can tell. Oriol isn't sure about that at all.

Jaantzen is listening to something through his earpiece. "Get her in the van," he says. "Gia's meeting us here."

"Boss?" Manu shares a quick look with Oriol.

Jaxie clears her throat. "But Blackheart — "

"Coeur is meeting us here, too."

Manu's sharing a look with Oriol. What the hell? Dueling with Blackheart isn't the way he'd been hoping to spend the rest of today.

"Let's get her in the van," Manu says.

In the van, Beni's slumped on one of the bench seats with his chin on his chest. He looks up groggily as Oriol and Manu lift Toshiyo in, and raises his hands.

"I'm on your team," Beni says. "Whoever the hell your team is now."

"Good to hear it," Manu says. "I think we're gonna need a good driver soon."

Beni sighs. "You all done shooting each other out there?"

"Probably not."

"I hate this job."

"Tell me about it. Keep an eye on her, and get ready to — "

Beside him, Oriol swears and spins back to face the main door to the garage. Manu hears the soft click of Oriol's rifle, the faint whine of Jaxie's pulse carbine. The sharp clack of Jaantzen's machine gun. He turns back to face the open door, aiming with his left pistol and handing his right back to Toshiyo.

"The red button on the side is the safety," he murmurs. "Don't shoot if I'm in the way."

"I can shoot a gun," she says, but her voice is shaking. He doesn't risk a glance back to see how she's doing.

A pair of burly bodyguards stalk through the door first, then the slim, dark silhouette Manu will never mistake.

Thala Coeur stares down the barrels of a quartet of weapons and smiles.

16

PAYOUT

"Willem."

Coeur waves back her bodyguards and steps into the center of the room. A half dozen barrels follow her. And she may be three to four and look unarmed herself, but Manu recognizes the assault carbines her bodyguards are carrying. Those bullets are made to pierce powered armor. A van door isn't going to do much to stop them. Nor will the light body armor he saw Oriol putting on back at the warehouse.

Coeur takes a slow, deliberate scan of the room, ignoring the pair of bodies but holding each person's gaze in turn. Her head's high, her shoulders loose, like she's walking into a bout she's planning to win. Thing with Coeur, though, she's not brash, she's not cocky. She wins because she plans to, not because she expects to. Manu gives her a faint nod when she meets his gaze, and he sees her nostrils flare, evaluating whether or not she can count him friend or foe.

Foe, bitch.

She turns to Jaantzen last. The gold-tipped ends of her braids clatter together as a handful of them slip off her shoulder.

"I thought we had a nice plan," she says to Jaantzen. "Didn't you think so?"

"Up until the part where you were planning to hang me up for the Alliance."

"Sorry about that, Willem. And I apologize for underestimating you."

"I don't expect you'll do it again."

A long, slow smile. Her gaze sweeps the room once more. "I misjudged your ability to inspire loyalty."

"Money can do that."

Money did that for Oriol and Jaxie, certainly — but Manu can hear Toshiyo's labored breathing behind him, thinks of Gia out there somewhere. Thinks about how he's just sided against the most dangerous woman in Bulari. No amount of money could have gotten him to make such a misguided move.

"Speaking of money." Coeur presses a button on her comm. Jaantzen's own chimes in his pocket. "You've got your cash, so bring in your gal and let's do some business." Her gaze cuts briefly to Sarah and Kai. "What do you say, we're even? Looks like we both lost people on this one."

"I'm not sure Kai was one of my people," Jaantzen says.

Coeur just shrugs. You don't get as far as she has and still have a sense of shame, Manu figures.

"But I would say we're even, Thala. I was in it for the job, you were in it for the goods. We've both gotten what we came in for. Except you didn't get a fall guy to distract the Alliance."

"That's fine. I have a plan B."

"Glad to hear you'll end up all right."

"My goods, Willem."

Her hand's at her side, drumming on her thigh low and casual. It might be an unconscious gesture on someone else, but both her guards are keeping one eye on it.

Manu does, too.

"Ms. Ravi," Jaantzen says. "Can you please ask Ms. Até to join us?" Coeur's nostrils flare at Toshiyo's name like she's scenting for hidden prey; her attention falls on the van behind Manu. The guard at her left is tuned to her motions like an augment mech on a factory line; he shifts to sweep his weapon over the van. His right eye is a mercury swirl and he's blinking strangely, like information is feeding into a contact lens. Could be his scope doubles as a scanner.

"Got it, boss," Toshiyo calls from the van. Manu can hear her tapping on her hand terminal, faint under the sound of her labored breathing.

"Giaconda is on her way," Jaantzen says.

And by on her way, he means she's been waiting in the wings for her dramatic cue.

"Got your goods, Thala."

Gia's voice comes from the doorway that leads farther into the office complex. She's got an iridescent case on a wheeled cart that looks like it was stolen from a hotel lobby.

Coeur breaks into a slow smile. "Thanks, sugar," she says.

Manu thinks he could live to one hundred and never again hear someone call Giaconda "Sugar."

"We'll just be on our way, and you can have your goods," says Jaantzen. "As you suggested, I think we can say we're even. But please take me off your list of available contractors in the future."

"I'd say I'll be taking a few people off my list," she says, gaze sweeping the room again. Again, her gaze stops briefly on Manu. He gives her another slight nod and she looks satisfied. Manu's attention is on the hand on her thigh. "You're free to go," Coeur says. "You have my word. Pleasure working with you, Willem."

"Wish I could say the same."

Jaantzen raises his chin to Gia, and she gives the cart a kick. It glides, clattering across the cracked cement floor.

Thala Coeur grins. She reaches for the handle with one hand; her other hand cuts a sharp arc. Her guards snap their rifles to squeeze out the rounds that'll end them all.

Manu squeezes his fist on the detonator hidden in his palm.

The room explodes.

Hornet tags are brilliant.

They're practically invisible to the naked eye, just a piece of explosive resin the size of Manu's thumbnail on a patch of transparent adhesive. A bit of ignition, a minuscule receiver. They're no grenade, shredding through the room with shrapnel. They're no dynamite. Really, the only way they'll kill you is if you have a bad heart and don't know they're coming.

But they're distracting as hell — especially when you've slapped a bunch up on big glass panes and shoddy electrical boxes.

He's timed the first wave a fraction of a second apart, so it sounds like a spray of gunfire coming from outside the building.

Coeur has a pistol in one hand, and her own round of bullets sends Manu and Jaantzen ducking for cover. Her bodyguards are slower to react — one has turned to the entrance as though to face a new threat from that direction. Jaxie drops him. Oriol drops the other.

"Don't shoot the case," Jaantzen bellows, and Manu pulls up at the last minute so his shot goes wide and shatters one of the plate windows he hadn't tagged. Coeur and her mystery case are silhouetted in a glittering hail of glass as she sprints back out the door.

Outside, Manu hears voices yelling. Coeur's guys? Police? He's not interested in finding out.

"I'd be a lot happier about the future if we'd gotten her, too," Oriol mutters.

"Time for a long vacation," Manu says.

"Goddammit, Manu," Gia yells.

"Wasn't that fun?" he yells back. "Handy, too."

"We can talk about fun later." She shoulders past him into the van. "Hey, Tosh. Hold on, babe. Beni, how you feeling, buddy? You ready to drive?" Beni stares at her with naked fear.

Outside, the voices are getting closer. Manu runs to cover

Jaantzen as he limps towards the van. Jaxie's joined him, driven by her natural lackey's instinct to protect the alpha, whoever that alpha may be. "Lotta guys out there," she says.

"Then let's head out the back," Jaantzen says. "I'm sending coordinates to your nav."

They pile into the van. Beni's in the driver's seat, eyes on Gia like she's a feral scrub hyena. Gia's got Toshiyo strapped to one of the benches and is waving some magic medical wand over her abdomen. "Nice job on the coag nanites, whoever thought of that."

"Oriol," Jaxie says. "How bulletproof is this thing?"

"Not very," Jaantzen says, checking his gun. "I hope your reflexes are recovered, Mr. Chav."

Beni just snorts. "Bitch can't steal my touch."

Gia laughs.

"Good to hear. Now let's drive."

Manu sets off his second round of hornet tags as Beni peels out of the garage, and just as a swarm of Coeur's thugs come piling in. This time — and he's proud of this one — a pair of tags have just enough power to sever a wire cable suspending a hoist. It drops, sags against the remaining cable, then twists free in a shriek of rusted metal-on-metal.

Beni swerves out of the way just in time, throwing them all against the wall of the van. Jaxie and Oriol are first to recover, firing out the windows at the gunmen who are still standing.

Gia hoists herself back to Toshiyo's side. "How many more of those do you have, asshole?" she growls at Manu.

"Zero more," Manu says. "Somebody wouldn't buy me any."

"Please add hornet tags as a permanent item on Mr. Juric's supply list," Jaantzen says.

"Noted with fucking objections, boss," Gia says.

Permanent item.

Oriol gives him a look, perfect eyebrow raised, and Manu almost says something to brush it off. But he doesn't have anything to prove to Oriol.

Jaantzen's watching him, and Manu gives the man a nod.

"Got it, boss," he says.

17

NEVER SAY 'AIN'T EVER'

Beni's handling skills seem to have recovered as quickly as he said they would, and within a few minutes they're in a nondescript office complex in the bad part of the North Bulari industrial district. Manu feels his soul shriveling just being in this part of town, which during the day is full of indentured office workers and the humming of official business: trade, infrastructure, construction. He doesn't understand what they do here, and he doesn't care.

Cheap adobe walls make the street feel like a desert canyon, cut off the view to the businesses behind, differentiated only by the address numbers and occasional business name stenciled on the sheetmetal gates. The better-kept businesses have painted their section of the wall, stopping sharply at the property line as if to say, Unlike those guys, we take pride in our business.

The wall around the old-fashioned accordion gate that

Jaantzen directs Beni to stop in front of is clearly owned by one of those guys, with paint scored back by sandstorms so badly that a lattice of cement blocks shows through the adobe in places. But when Jaantzen gets out to palm the lock, the gate sparks faintly as the invisible energy shield around the place shimmers to off.

A pack rat scurries out of the wall.

Inside is a short driveway and a soulless office building.

"We're safe here," Jaantzen calls, and Manu jumps out to help him secure the accordion gate once more. His scalp tingles as the energy field sizzles back on.

Gia seems to know the place — she directs Oriol and Jaxie to carry Toshiyo into the office building, orders Beni to come with them so he can lie down. No one barks orders at Manu, so he steps back to the van to start sorting through the chaos of gear this little adventure has produced.

"Mr. Juric, if you have a moment."

Manu gingerly brushes shards of broken glass off his gear bag, which is mercifully sealed. "Yeah, boss." The word comes out without him meaning it to.

Last time Manu was alone with Jaantzen, he was plotting how to get a knife between the man's shoulder blades and get out alive. Now?

Manu's not sure where they stand now.

"What is your estimation of me?" Jaantzen asks.

It's not the question Manu was expecting. He frowns at the man. He's studied him for weeks, spent plenty of time watching for weaknesses these past few days. His estimation has shifted, but he's not sure when. Probably before he even made the decision not to kill him out on the balcony.

"You're not what I expected," he says. Jaantzen waits, watching him. "Kai, that's more who I expected based on what I heard about you. You've got a reputation for being someone who hires disposable crew — who is disposable. Which I guess is why Coeur thought she could hang you out to dry."

Manu's thinking. He's not sure how to say all this. "Where'd you find Toshiyo?" he asks instead.

Jaantzen's expression darkens, a storm hovering over his brow. "By reputation," he says. "I was looking to hire a permanent ops tech to handle security and surveillance, and word came about a tech genius at a mining corporation."

"So you bought her indenture."

Manu says it wrong, deliberate, and sees Jaantzen balk like the idea is distasteful.

"I paid off her indenture," he says. "Then I hired Ms. Ravi on retainer to help me when I need it."

"Retainer?" Manu asks, frowning. Most bosses in Bulari run their crew as indentures or pay them per job.

"I don't work with anyone who can't walk away, but I don't want to scrounge for my team each time."

Jaantzen's watching him now, gaze steady and even.

Manu breaks first; he nods and shifts as though he's scanning the compound. "And Gia? She's a trip."

"Gia and I have a long history," Jaantzen says. "I don't require her services often."

"And Kai?"

"Kai was from the old way of doing things. Someone I'd contracted with many times in the past, but never trusted. I need people I can trust, Mr. Juric."

"Understood."

"I can offer you a monthly retainer, plus overtime and a bonus for the more dangerous jobs. In exchange I would prefer you work solely for me."

"Join your crew." Manu tilts his head. "Your crew's got a bad rap. That's the other thing I know about you."

"It does, and for understandable reasons." Jaantzen clears his throat. "And I would like you to help me change that."

Manu blinks, not sure at first if he's heard correctly.

"Me?"

"I've been watching you. You read every person on this job like a book, and you played them just as well as you needed. I'd planned to kill you during our first conversation, yet by the end of it, I'd hired you."

"I appreciate that."

"I saw you bolster Toshiyo's confidence when we needed her. You've defused Kai and Beni." He gave a faint smile. "You've even made Gia laugh. You're a decent fighter, but I can find a dozen of those on any street corner in any slum. What I need is someone who can help me build a team."

Somewhere down the line, Manu's already made the decision. He shrugs. "Course."

"You're not going to negotiate?"

"We can talk about money later."

"Coeur will probably try to kill you if you work for me."

"I'm already on her shit list. Probably got a better chance working with you than wandering out on my own."

Jaantzen nods slowly. "What about the others?"

Manu knows who he means: Oriol, Beni, Jaxie. He takes them in order of easiness.

"Jaxie's bad news on a good day," he says. "I wouldn't trust her to water my jadau plant while I was on vacation without sniffing around to find somebody who'd pay her more to let it die instead. But let her run back to Sylla with her cash and she'll be too embarrassed at taking the pay to bring any fight back to you.

"Beni'll do the job well, but he won't put his life on the line for you. You knew that. The thing I'd watch if I were you is I get the sense he holds a grudge, and he's not happy about what Gia did to him. And you, by extension."

Manu feels bad saying it, knows it's probably a death sentence. "Let me talk to him and be sure," he adds. If he senses that Beni will be a threat to his new crew, he can take care of it himself.

Jaantzen nods slowly. "And Mr. Sina?"

Ah, now there's a blind spot, if Manu's not careful. "Oriol doesn't seem interested in anybody else's drama. He's not curious, and he doesn't talk if he doesn't need to. The man's a pro."

"Would he make a good addition to my crew?"

"Oriol?" He's the type of no-nonsense person with a put-together life that Manu has always been drawn to. It would be nice to keep working alongside him, but Manu has to be honest with Jaantzen — and himself. "Nah, boss. He plays for his own team. Keep his number, though."

Jaantzen nods, and his gaze shifts past Manu's shoulder. Manu turns to see that Oriol has come back out of the office building, is leaning lazy shoulders against the adobe wall.

"I presume you'll have it," Jaantzen says. He claps Manu

on the shoulder. "I'm going to go see Toshiyo. Keep an eye out."

"Sure thing, boss."

Manu watches him walk away, then crosses the driveway. "Hey, man."

Oriol tilts his head to look at him, a faint smile on his lips. "Hope you asked for what you're worth," he says.

Manu shrugs. What he's worth is a relative number. What Jaantzen's worth to him is even more so. He's not worried about cash. Besides, he doesn't want to talk about it, not with Oriol. "What are your plans?" he asks. "You got your pay, did your job. On to the next adventure?"

"Gonna lie low," he says.

Manu's watching, wondering if he's been put out of the picture now that he's chosen sides. Now that he's not so cool and smooth.

And as though he can read Manu's mind, Oriol's sardonic smile cracks briefly into the genuine thing. "I ain't ever working with you again, man."

"Never say 'ain't ever,'" Manu says, and Oriol just shakes his head. "And besides. You just said you don't have plans to work for a minute, anyway. Not until this whole thing blows over." He tests his luck, leans against the wall a couple inches from Oriol. "I heard you were planning a little vacation."

"Could be."

"Need some company?"

Oriol smiles. "Could be." Oriol's gaze trails downwards as though considering, then his thumb hooks into Manu's waistband, tugging him a fraction of an inch closer. His other hand reaches into Manu's pocket to pull out his comm. Manu's hip is on fire.

Oriol types his information into Manu's comm, hands it back.

"Now you know how to get ahold of me."

"I was born knowing how to get ahold a person," Manu says with a lift of an eyebrow. "I'll show you if you want."

"You can't come if you're gonna make a joke out of every-thing," Oriol says, then reddens. Manu starts to laugh. "Dammit, man. I already regret giving you my number."

"I'll make sure that regret's short-lived," Manu says. He pats the comm in his pocket. "When we go on vacation," he adds.

Life's about to get good.

ACKNOWLEDGMENTS

I owe a huge debt of gratitude to a number of people for their support and patience as I worked on *Negative Return*.

To every person who left a review on my last two books, or took the time to tell me how much you liked them in person, *THANK YOU!!!* You all have no idea how much that kept me going. Especially Kristin Koontz, who despite my horror at it keeps introducing me to people by saying, "This is my friend Jessie and she's an author."

Thank you to my husband, Robert Kittilson, for brainstorming plot elements with me for hours on end — and for being blunt about when an idea sounded boring. You were correct every time.

Thank you thank you to Andrea Rangel, Elizabeth Mitchell, and Kathy Kwak for being willing to read my first drafts, and for the excellent feedback. You ladies are amazing.

Finally, thanks to Fiona Jade (fionajaydemedia.com) for the cover design, and to the eagle-eyed Kyra Freestar (Bridge Creek Editing) for the phenomenal editing.

ABOUT THE AUTHOR

Jessie Kwak is a freelance writer and novelist living in Portland, Oregon. When she's not working with B2B marketers, you can find her scribbling away on her latest novel, riding her bike to the brewpub, or sewing something fun.

Learn more about me (and get free books!) by signing up for my mailing list at jessiekwak.com.

ALSO BY JESSIE KWAK

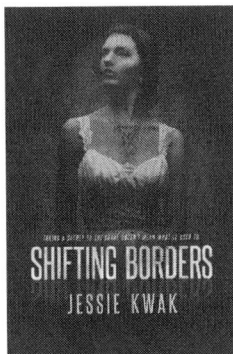

It's been years since the Ramos sisters have been close, but when Patricia is accidentally possessed by Valeria's dead boyfriend, Marco, they have one last shot at working out their differences. But with a drug smuggling gang hot on their heels, will they have time to heal their relationship?

From Razorgirl Press. Available in print and ebook on Amazon.

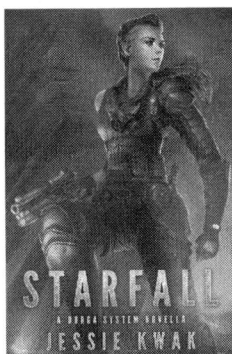

Starla Dusai is fifteen, deaf — and being held as an enemy combatant by the Indiran Alliance. Willem Jaantzen is a notorious crime lord about to end a fearsome vendetta — and most probably his life. When he learns his goddaughter has been captured by the Alliance, will he be able to save her? And her, him?

Available in print, ebook, and audiobook on Amazon.

Made in the USA
Columbia, SC
17 November 2017